Incident

AT

Happy Valley

© 2023 Tom Fleming. All rights reserved. No part of this book may be copied or reproduced in any form without written permission from the author, except for short excerpts used in reviews.

ISBN: 978-1-938394-84-3
Library of Congress Control Number: 2023919050

Great Life Press
Goffstown, New Hampshire 03045
greatlifepress.com

This book is fiction. The characters, plot, businesses, or events described are fictitious and not meant to resemble any particular person or place. For the most part, they are figments of the author's imagination and observations. Any similarities to persons living or dead are purely coincidental.

Incident AT Happy Valley

Tom Fleming

Acknowledgments

Thanks to Doc Wakey, Squeaky Green, Linda and Katie for their
confidence, encouragement, and support.
Special thanks to Grace Peirce.

Dedication

This book is dedicated to my friends, David and Jane Berg, campground owners extraordinaire. My many visits to their campground, watching the style, enthusiasm, and vigor in which they managed it, were always a pleasure. It gave me, and I'm sure, other visitors, the true meaning of Wicked Good camping. My many years of law enforcement experience are incorporated into the contents of this story. The rest is from just plain imagination, a little help from Doc, and maybe my friend . . . the ghost.

Happy Valley

I made my initial visit to Happy Valley campground several years ago. I was reluctant to go, which is not unusual for me, but I finally gave in to my son's insistence. He was adamant that I see the place. Even after agreeing to go, I was not sure if I'd made the right decision, but his description of the campground and the people that owned and operated it, intrigued me. Camping is not a new thing for me. I have camped for more than twenty years, in either tents or campers, in rain and sun, enjoying it immensely.

Upon arrival at Happy Valley, all visitors and or campers must check in at the main office, where they are greeted by the owners. My son, who had been there several times before, introduced me to them. The man appeared to be a laid back, friendly gentleman, who immediately made me feel welcome and at ease. That was a relief for me. I must admit my first impression of this man was, wow, I really like this guy. It was obvious, as friendly as he appeared, he was a no nonsense right-in-your-face type of man; his eyes told the whole story. I pride myself on being able to read people's faces, and that's exactly how I like it. Usually when I'm impressed, I won't show it, but instantly I knew I wouldn't mind getting to know him better. There was no doubt in my mind he and I would get along fine.

On the other hand, his wife appeared very nice but a little more reserved. She was pleasant, friendly, and business-like, but there was something else I couldn't put my finger on. It was evident they were a team by the way they reacted to questions, without looking at each other. I'd have to think about her—she was going to be a challenge. I had a strange feeling that she and I wouldn't get along very well, and I wasn't sure why.

As time went by, I was really getting to know the gentleman. Then he passed away suddenly, which was a shock to everyone who knew him. His wife, to no one's surprise, took over running the campground without missing a beat. I'm sure the emotional toll was tremendous, but she never let it show and it was business as usual.

One sunny afternoon I was having a friendly discussion with a friend that I fondly refer to as Doc, about the different behaviors a campground seems to bring out in people—not unheard of when you have a diverse group congregated in a relatively small area. Their reactions, or little quirks, become more noticeable, some good and some bad. Everyone seems to have some sort of an agenda—mostly to have a good time. I looked at my friend and said, "You know, Doc, with a little imagination I could write a book about this place," to which he responded with a big smile, "Then do it." That's how this book came about.

As for this campground, it's bustling, and getting better each day. I'm more than thrilled that my son insisted I visit. I love this place and the great bunch of people that live here. As for the lady that I felt would be a challenge, well she still is, but regardless, I fell in love with her and her campground. What else can I say?

~ Part 1 ~

Prologue

In the hustle and bustle of this modern world, people from every walk of life are striving to find the perfect way to get some relaxation, or one might say, get away from it all. That, of course, could be considered a very broad statement, because each person's definition of relaxation is different. For example, it could mean swimming, boating, drinking with friends, curling up with a good book, lying on the beach soaking up the sun, or going to a ballgame. There are so many things to choose from these days. Here's one to consider. How about the adventure of going on a camping trip? Just picture yourself doing a little hiking, or just taking a leisurely walk with a friend along a shade-covered path, enjoying nature at its best. Many campgrounds, regardless of size, offer a small lake or a pool, where you could swim or sunbathe. Just imagine when your fun-filled day finally comes to its end, you could sit around a campfire and toast marshmallows, sing songs, look at the stars or maybe even tell scary ghost stories.

Taking into consideration any of these options, it may surprise you to find that camping was the first choice of a large number of people surveyed. It appears that sitting around a campfire might be one of America's favorite pastimes.

Now assuming this little pep talk about camping has piqued your interest and you have decided to try a little camping, there are several things you might consider. Finding the right mode to suit your particular camping needs may be the first challenge. You could choose a tent—some can be simple and just provide shelter from the weather and the bugs. Others are more elaborate, with windows and screened porches, but also a little harder to set up, which could be a problem if a sudden rain shower arrives before you finish assembling it. Then there's the tent trailer—easy to move, more modern than a tent, and a little more costly. You might consider the majestic motorhome, which contains everything, including the kitchen sink. Some of the larger motorhomes are like a self-contained house.

The next consideration is what your adventure will cost. Since camping has become so popular, the industry for manufacturing campers and motorhomes has exploded. This has provided a large variety of campers and motorhomes in all different sizes, shapes, styles, and price ranges. This expansive availability gives you endless potential on how far you can travel, what you can bring with you, and ultimately where you can go.

Now that we're on the subject of where you can go, let me suggest a great place I am familiar with. I was there at the beginning stages of its development, and watched it grow into one of the highest-rated seasonal places to visit. I frequently make return visits there whenever I have the opportunity. If you visit you might even see me at one time or another. I would say that you have never really experienced pure perfection until you have enjoyed a glorious summer morning at Happy Valley Campground in southern Maine.

Happy Valley is regarded as one of Maine's elite campgrounds. It boasts over one hundred campsites, some permanent, with park model campers spaciously located throughout several hundred well-maintained, completely fenced-in acres. Along with the permanent sites, there is an area for transient campers to come and spend a few days or weeks, and a secluded area set aside strictly for tenting. All the sites, except the tent sites, have sewage, water, and electric hook-ups available. The streets are paved and dotted with fashionable streetlamps along the way. There's a pristine bath house with a laundry attached, an in-ground heated saltwater pool, a playground for children, and a bandstand for weekly concerts. A large building at the entrance houses the main office, a store, and recreational hall. In addition to this, it's located within a mile of the beautiful Maine seashore, featuring sun-swept beaches and delightful dining. The campground resembles a small village, where one could easily live year-round. Of course, now and then you might hear the occasional rattle of pots and pans for preparing breakfast, smell bacon cooking or fresh coffee brewing, and maybe the squeals and laughter of children, or an occasional dog barking—all this under a bright sunny sky as blue as a robin's egg. Who could ask for anything more?

But like all good things or places you might visit or stay, Happy Valley also has its ups and downs. On the upside you could sit around your camp, and at any given time, watch a cast of characters unknowingly perform in front of you. There are times this group could make television's Comedy Central® seem like a Peanuts® cartoon.

Unwittingly, these characters seem to have brought their hopes, fears, and problems with them on their vacation. Deep inside they believe some miracle will happen while they're here, making everything that's been bothering them go away. Then amazingly, they will head back home after a few days or weeks worry-free. One could only hope this were possible.

One example of this cast of characters is a woman named Julie, a good-looking blonde about thirty years old, who walks the two miles of campground road seven or eight times every day, as fast as she can. Julie never stops to talk to anyone. She just walks, wearing a big smile on her face. Occasionally she looks back to see if she is being followed. She is on a mission and can't be late.

We can put her right up there with Bob, the former road race guy. Bob's a middle-aged, friendly, good-looking man in fine physical condition. He runs at least five miles a day on the same route as Julie. Maybe he's looking for the checkered flag of life or trying to catch up with Julie. The Lord only knows, but they appear to be happy, and I guess that's what's important. Then we have my personal favorites: the campground queens. This group of five or six ladies, depending on the weather, walk, talk, gawk, squawk, and without question gossip about everyone and everything they see. Nothing is sacred. No need for a newspaper, radio, or television with them around—they do it all.

This campground is also unique in regards to its design, one portion has permanent sites with park model trailers of every type and style, scattered tastefully throughout. These trailers would be incomplete without the owners with attitudes to match. I'm sure you've probably figured out by now, our cast of characters all belong to this group. Nevertheless, putting all this together with its surroundings, you get the picturesque setting of a small happy campground, without confusion or drama. That is, except for the gossip conjured up by the campground queens, that spreads like butter and syrup on a hot pancake. It makes life more interesting.

—1—

October mornings in Maine are traditionally clear, bright, cool, and sunny. There's just enough chill in the air to wear a jacket or sweatshirt and snuggle up to a hot cup of coffee.

The campground closes early in October and the air is filled with activity. Now and then you might hear other campers that have to leave early, reluctantly putting things away preparing to leave—many of them waving and calling, "goodbye, stay healthy, see you next year," as they slowly pass by.

But you're not leaving today. There's plenty of time to start a campfire, sit and have another cup of coffee, while waiting for some breakfast. You're certainly in no hurry for this to end, but we know, unfortunately like everything else, things are not always this perfect. Let me give you an example.

There was that rainy cool early October morning. Fall was in the air, bringing its chill. Everyone was busy packing their belongings and hooking up their campers, preparing for the long trip home. The campground would be closing the next day and all the campers must be gone. Hugs, laughter, and goodbyes were in the air. Who would've suspected that all at once this blissful happiness would come to a screeching halt.

The mother of a teenage girl has just come to the conclusion that her daughter is missing. The girl, whose name is Susan, had been camping with her family in a secluded section of the campground. This particular area is set aside exclusively for tenting, located amongst the trees, adjacent to the campground fence line. It's tastefully situated far enough away from the mobile homes and trailers to give tenters a space with privacy.

The girl's parents had no idea she was missing when they prepared breakfast; she was sort of a loner and was always late for everything. They assumed she had gone to the bathhouse to wash and gave it no mind. After a short while, the mother thought it was taking much longer than usual for the girl to wash up and went to the bathhouse to check on her. Unable to find her right away, she decided to make a more thorough check of the bathhouse and the immediate area. She then decided to go back and check the girl's tent, along the way stopping to ask other campers if they had seen her. Everyone she asked told her they had not, so she hurried back to the girl's tent to find it empty. The girl was gone and it appeared she had taken her backpack, cell phone, and iPad with her. After finding no sign of the girl, the panicked mother raced to the campground front office to advise the owner of the situation and ask for assistance.

The campground owner, Katie Burns, has a heart of gold, the toughness of a truck driver, and her finger on the pulse of the entire campground. Katie's husband David had unexpectedly passed away during the winter leaving her to run the campground by herself. She has taken this huge responsibility in stride, making it look easy.

After listening to the mother explain that she couldn't find her daughter and the steps she'd taken to locate her, Katie jumped into action.

The first call she made was to her chief of security, a hard-nosed by-the-book retired cop by the name of Tommy J. McGrath. The "J" stood for Jesse, and that's the name most people called him. Katie had complete confidence in Jesse and for good reason. Jesse had been a police officer in Massachusetts and New Hampshire for almost thirty years. Unfortunately he was forced to retire after being shot in the knee by a fleeing shoplifter, leaving him with 10% limp and 90% attitude. There wasn't much he hadn't seen or done. He stood about five-foot-eight inches, weighed 210 pounds, and was as rugged as a fullback. Jesse held a black belt in Karate that he hardly had to rely on due to a devastating right hook that set many a tough guy on their backside.

When Jesse arrived and was informed of the situation, he quickly looked at the clock and asked if any campers had left yet that morning. Katie told him nobody had left as of yet, and no one was scheduled to arrive, the camp register was closed for the year. This meant once the campers on site had departed—the gates would be closed for the season.

Jesse thought for a few minutes and then told Katie to temporarily close the gates, and not to let anyone leave. He further advised her to call the sheriff's office, tell them about the problem, and request they send some deputies over.

That being taken care of, he decided to get some more backup just in case. He put in a call to his good friend, MJ Davis, a special crimes investigator. MJ and he had worked many cases together before.

MJ was a semi-retired cop who was assigned to a special undercover initiative set up by the governor of New Hampshire, called the Internet Crimes Against Children Task Force (ICAC). He stood about six foot, weighed 220 pounds and was all muscle. He was also a martial arts student with more belts than a lumber yard sawmill motor. He was his own boss more or less, and answered only to the governor. MJ had a partner—a two-year-old mixed breed Golden Lab named Neiko—as big as a small bear and as cuddly as a kitten. Neiko's specialty, among other things, was his ability to sniff out hidden electronic devices used by individuals to film, record, and exploit children. MJ was recognized by the governor as a top-notch investigator. For that reason, the governor picked him for his task force, in spite of immense political pressure from the good old boy network to choose one of their preferred cronies. But once the governor had made up his mind about something, the chances of changing it were almost unheard of, and MJ was his pick.

Jesse and MJ had a good working relationship despite MJ's propensity to instigate problems, many that might be well enough left alone. Some of the older officers that knew him referred to him as a shit magnet, because often when MJ got involved in a case, that's when the shit would start. He was also known to be almost unstoppable until he got what he was after. Sometimes Jesse would step in to run interference, hoping the case would be solved before they both would be looking for work in Northern Siberia.

Jesse apprised MJ of the situation at the campground, and asked if there was any chance he could break away from what he was doing and give him a hand. The response was just what he hoped.

"When and where do you want me? You name it I'll be there," was MJ's reply.

This was one of the many times Jesse was glad MJ was available to help him. His "don't tell me how to do my job" attitude toward the talking heads and know-it-all brass would give them a little working room if outside agencies tried to intervene.

The towns surrounding Happy Valley are small in population, but not in area. Most have no police departments to speak of, so the sheriff's department is the law of the land, and I do mean land. They were spread so thin trying to cover so many towns, it was ridiculous. Some of these deputies would work twelve- and fourteen-hour shifts daily for weeks at a time, leaving little doubt they were worn out from lack of sleep. It was rumored that Ichabod Crane had a better chance of catching the headless horseman than these deputies would have at catching a burglar. The last thing they needed was a missing person to look for. Unfortunately, they had to be called and advised of the situation. Jesse and his crew had no authority when it came to law enforcement.

Just delaying the campers from leaving could have some bad repercussions if someone complained, and Jesse knew it.

While he awaited the deputy's arrival, Jesse decided to take advantage of a few assets he had at his disposal. There were a few trustworthy maintenance people working at Happy Valley who could be useful. They had all been given a complete background check before being hired, some were more reliable than others. Jesse gathered them together, split them up into groups, and sent them out to search the area.

Campers on a whole are a pretty good group of people, all out to have a good time rain or shine. They are from every walk of life—doctors, lawyers, teachers, construction workers, students, the average housewife, families, friends, and relatives spending some time in the great outdoors. Interacting with each other as if they have known each other all their lives.

But sometimes, mixed among these happy campers, there were always a few that you had to watch—referred to by street cops as "leaks," symbolizing a leak in society, like a leak in a dike, or a weak spot you can't trust. They were usually, but not always, easy for a cop or a trained investigator to recognize. They, of course, considered themselves to be upstanding citizens, but in reality they were parasites, always slithering, watching, waiting for a chance to take advantage of someone's good nature. When the time is right, they make their move and capitalize on a good or bad situation. Without doubt, there were a few here at the campground and they would be watched closely.

Fortunately, Jesse had another ace in his pocket. In the center of this beautiful campground lived a low profile, guitar-playing gun nut named Doc. He lived there with his good-looking girlfriend, a nurse by the name of Peachy Keene. Doc stands about six-foot-six and weighs about 280, without an ounce of fat. Although he keeps an extremely low profile, he is always watchful, listening and making mental notes of anything he thinks is different or out of the ordinary. He's smart, trustworthy, honest, and dependable. The only place you usually find these qualities all in one place is as words in the dictionary.

There were other things about Doc that Jesse was aware of and he doubted anyone else at the campground knew. There are some things you might know about a particular individual that you never reveal, especially about a loyal friend. Doc is, strangely enough, known in a certain government agency as "Mr. Smith"—a man of many talents—Jesse thought with a smile. Doc was also a former campground owner and developer. It was common knowledge that Doc could tell you about every nook and cranny of the campground, including where the water, electric, and sewer lines were located. He was a walking encyclopedia when it came to the campground.

Many times Jesse would stop by and run his personal problems by Doc. It made him feel good to get a different perspective on things, rather than rely on the usual cop line of thinking. He had a feeling he would be reaching out to the good doctor, probably sooner than later.

Jesse wanted to keep this whole case as low key as possible. First and foremost he had to be sure there was a missing girl, and second, avoid panic and interference from the other campers. Although the campers meant well, sometimes they were more of a hindrance than a help.

His next step was to ask Katie to request the sheriff's department put a tracking dog on standby just in case. Then he said to himself, *get MJ and go meet the parents of the allegedly missing girl. Let's be sure she's missing and try to find out exactly what's going on.*

When they arrived at the missing girl's campsite, the parents introduced themselves as Ken and Barbie Jones from Brewer, Massachusetts. Ken was a pleasant, rugged-looking man. He told Jesse and MJ that he had been employed as a heavy equipment operator for the State of Massachusetts, since his discharge from the military. He explained that the family had been planning this trip to Happy Valley for a couple of years—it was their long-awaited vacation. Barbie, Ken's wife, was a slim, pleasant woman with long brown hair and a charming smile that could light up a room. Barbie told Jesse and MJ that she and Ken had met while they were in the military together and were married shortly after being discharged. She further told them she also was employed by the State of Massachusetts as a special needs school teacher.

The couple were visibly shaken, as was their younger daughter Lilly, a boisterous young girl about twelve years old with blonde curly hair and a mile-long smile. The couple had little information to add to the initial report of their missing daughter. Barbie explained that while she was making breakfast for the family, their sixteen-year-old daughter Susan just seemed to disappear, and was nowhere to be found.

"Tell us about Susan," MJ said to Barbie.

"Well," Barbie said, "Susan—we call her Sue—is sixteen, about five-foot-two inches tall, and weighs about 105 pounds. She has long blonde hair, hazel eyes, and walks with a slight limp."

"Why the limp?" MJ asked. "Was it an injury or birth defect?"

"It was the result of an auto accident when she was very young," she said. "It's not a bad limp but it is noticeable and she's very self-conscious about it."

"What about boyfriends or girlfriends?" MJ asked.

"Only a few girlfriends. No boys I know of. She likes to keep to herself and is very quiet. She hardly even talks. We have to drag things out of her sometimes."

"But Mom, what about that phone call she got yesterday?" Lilly quickly interjected.

"Oh that," Barbie said. "It was only spam or a wrong number I'm sure."

"But Mom, it really seemed to upset her. I could see it in her eyes."

"Where's her phone now?" Jesse asked. "We'd like to see it."

"It's gone, along with her iPad," Barbie said.

"Okay, besides the phone and iPad, what else is missing?" MJ asked.

"Just what she had on. We didn't see her go to the washroom. I'd have to guess jeans, sneakers, and a t-shirt. Her blue backpack that she keeps her silly drawings in is also gone."

"What kind of drawings?" Jesse asked.

"Just sketches of animals and people," Barbie said.

Jesse checked his watch and determined it had been approximately forty-five minutes since he had initially been notified about the missing girl. The search party had no luck at all and were backtracking in hopes they would find something they missed. Already he knew time was not on his side. "What else can you tell us?" he asked her.

"I can't think of anything," she said. "There have been no family problems with Sue and she seemed to be having a great time camping. There is one thing. I don't know what bearing it may have, but Sue is adopted. We adopted her when she was a small child. Her parents were killed in the same auto accident that left her with a limp."

The two investigators looked at each other. "We have to talk. Later." Jesse said to MJ.

MJ nodded and left Jesse with Ken and Barbie to go directly to the rec hall to organize a second search party. Upon his arrival, he called on a lead worker named Rick Smith to be in charge. Rick was a former Airborne Army Ranger that Jesse had handpicked to work at the camp. They had served together as military advisers during the 1960s in Vietnam. He was considered the most trusted and thorough of the workers. MJ told Rick to divide the group up as he saw fit and to begin searching the campground—all the buildings, sheds, and campers.

He also advised Rick that anyone who refused to have their

camper searched without a warrant was to be left alone. He told him to leave a maintenance worker at that particular camp until a warrant could be secured. MJ knew that he did not really need a warrant and he could probably convince them that under the colors of the public safety rule he did not need permission.

The public safety rule gives a law enforcement officer who has a reasonable belief that someone is in imminent danger, the right to enter a residence. But in this particular situation, MJ wanted to avoid bad feelings with the campers, wanting them to believe they were helping the search party. You get more with honey than salt, he thought.

The day was drawing near its end, it had been about eight hours since Jesse had received the original report. The rain was really starting to come down along with an occasional rumble of thunder and a flash of lightning. Just what we need, Jesse thought sarcastically, this shit won't help the dog if we call one in.

Meanwhile MJ and Neiko were doing their own kind of canvas of the campground. MJ was relentless once he started an investigation. He was sure someone must have heard or seen something. Sometimes just the right question would shake it out of them and shake is what he intended to do.

He decided to start with the transient campers so they could be sent on their way without further delay. He took Rocky, the camp chief of maintenance, a rugged tough-looking guy. Rocky was a retired semi-pro boxer, whose birth name was Eugene Campbell. He was given the nickname Rocky for his ability to hardly flinch when being pounded on by other fighters. His appearance alone was enough to make you think twice before refusing to cooperate. He was also a pot-stirrer and a gossip. Therefore having him out with the investigator was a good idea, in that he wouldn't be running his mouth all over camp about the investigation. Along with Neiko, the two would check every camper and vehicle inside and out. Neiko would identify any electronics and they would be checked to be sure they didn't belong to Sue. Then they would take photos of the owner's identification and addresses and send them on their way. Fortunately, there would be no new campers arriving due to the fact the campground was scheduled to close the next day. Once they eliminated the transients they could concentrate on the permanent campers.

MJ cautioned everyone that after they questioned the campers about the missing girl, to be sure and let them be on their way. There had been no crime committed and they had no authority to detain them.

Meanwhile, after finishing with Barbie and Ken, Jesse stormed into the office asking Katie, "Where the hell are the damn deputies, Dunkin' donuts?"

Katie looked at him and said nothing, her return look said it all. Finally, she spoke. "Just calm down. There's been a bad accident on Route 1 and they will probably be tied up all night. Looks like we're on our own for quite a while."

Jesse sat down at the table with his head in his hands, remembering the time several years ago when a three-year-old child was missing. In the nick of time she was found down by the river, behind the campground. At least this one is sixteen he thought, and a six-foot chain link fence had been installed around the camp. It was still a hard thing to shake, and he wished he could have a good stiff drink right about then.

Just before dark enveloped the campground, MJ, Neiko, Rick, and Rocky all met with Katie and Jesse to advise them that the last camper had been inspected and sent on its way, leaving only the permanent residents to check.

As luck would have it, that narrowed things down considerably. Most of the permanent campers had left days ago, leaving only the empty camps. It was decided that all the crews should go back to their homes, get some food and rest, and start fresh in the morning.

There were several reasons for this decision. The missing girl was old enough to fend for herself if necessary. Also it would have been almost impossible for her to have left the campground between the time she went to the bathhouse and the time she was reported missing. There were too many people moving about for her to slip out unnoticed. In addition to this, she did have some clothes, her cell phone and iPad with her. At least that's what her parents had initially reported. Taking all this into consideration, Jesse had a gut feeling she was somewhere on the property, possibly hiding, but why? With all this in mind, starting fresh in the morning with the permanent residents was the logical thing to do.

The gate would be guarded and all the security cameras around the camp would be activated and recording. Security patrols would be doubled all night—even a mouse would have trouble moving without being seen or stopped. After handing out assignments to the maintenance men that had not been on the original search team, the others were sent home and told to return at 6:30 in the morning. Jesse called MJ over and quietly said, "I think it's time you, me, and Neiko pay the Doc a visit."

To which MJ responded, "It's about time."

The three of them slowly made their way around the campground enroute to Doc's camp, listening and looking for any sign of the girl as they walked. Jesse and MJ bounced what ifs and whys off each other as they walked, hoping to make sense of the whole situation. Jesse told MJ of his gut feeling about the girl—that she was still there, either being held against her will or in hiding. He was not surprised that MJ's response in return was the same. Jesse smiled and thought to himself, great minds travel in the same circle, now if we can just put it all together.

Just as they rounded a corner in the lower part of the camp, sometimes referred to as Gossip Central, there was a flash of lightning and MJ saw what appeared to be someone ducking behind a camp. He took off running in that direction with Neiko leading the way. By the time Jesse caught up, MJ had the answer to what he thought he saw. Neiko had someone pinned to the ground squirming in the mud trying to get free.

"Well . . . look who we have here," Jesse said, as he shone his kel light in the person's face. It was Howard Wang, one of the camp's full-time residents. Howie, as he was referred to, was a camp handyman of sorts that on occasion would help Katie out. He was a small skinny man with a beard and, as Jesse would say, shifty eyes. "What the hell are you doing out here? You know we have this place on lockdown. I saw you in the storage room earlier when we were discussing it, so don't try to deny it."

Howie brushed himself off and said, "You guys know me, I was trying to help. I thought I saw someone run along the fence line over there and was going to follow them."

"Which direction was the person running?" MJ asked, as he looked all around trying to shield the rain from his face.

"Down toward the fence line in Gossip Central I think," Howie said. "I'm not sure—the lightning flashed and I jumped back, and then the dog jumped me."

"If you want to help," Jesse said, "Get your ass home and stay there. Don't let us catch you out again tonight."

MJ looked at Jesse after Howie left and said, "I don't like it. He's a strange guy. Let's check the fence line. Come on, Neiko."

After about forty-five minutes of trudging through the wet grass with the lightning dancing all around them they finished checking the fence in the area Howie sent them.

"I'm soaked and now I dislike that guy even more."

"I know," Jesse said. "I've always had a bad feeling about him. He reminds me of a little parasite, but remember just last week there was a report of a guy walking the fence looking in camper windows. We can't take any chances. You never know."

Just then Jesse's phone rang and it was Katie. "I've been

trying to get you," she said, "but the rain is interfering with the signal. The deputies arrived a while ago and are talking to Barbie and Ken, it seems pretty intense, so you may want to come back."

"Nothing we can do, Katie, it's their show now," Jesse said.

"The lead man made that quite evident," she replied. "He said you have no authority to hold the campers and they can leave when they want. His men will do what needs to be done. Furthermore he said if you interfere you will be arrested. I overheard him tell one of the deputies their next plan is talking to the owner of the campground across the street. But best of all, she laughed, it's Billy-Bob Benson from York County who's leading the investigation. Thought you might want to know." She was still laughing as she hung up.

"Oh shit," Jesse said to MJ. "It's Barney Fife and his gang. Let's go to Doc's and get a drink."

Upon their arrival, Doc opened the door and greeted them. "I expected you guys before this. What took you so long?"

"Nice to see you, too," Jesse responded. "What's to drink?"

The Doc poured them each a large vodka and tonic, gave an ice cube to Neiko, then motioned for them to sit.

"Okay," he said. "Let's hear it."

Jesse gave Doc a rundown of what had happened, only to have him say, "I know all that stuff—where do you stand as of now?"

Jesse should have known the eyes and the ears of the camp were already on top of it. MJ told the Doc what he had found out and that they had planned to finish in the morning, "but things may have changed," he said with a smile. "The deputies have arrived and will take the lead."

Doc asked who the deputies were that would be taking the case over, and after a pause Jesse told him. Doc just rolled his eyes and said, "Oh shit, no wonder you needed a drink."

MJ and Jesse told Doc about running into Howie and the

story he had told them about seeing someone behind the camp.

"We really don't know about this guy's story, but can't ignore it," MJ said.

"You're right about that!" Doc replied. "I don't trust that guy and never have in the twenty years I've known him."

"I don't know, Doc," Jesse said. "I have a gut feeling this mess is close to home and that girl is here somewhere. I know gut feelings don't solve cases, it's facts and evidence that do, but there's something nagging me I can't shake. Well, besides that, we better get back to the office and give Katie a break from the deputies' dog and pony show."

Just as they started to leave and MJ had stepped out the door, Doc pulled Jesse back by the shoulder and whispered, "go with the gut."

MJ and Jesse decided they would split up and take two different routes back to the office. MJ and Neiko would go through the tent area while Jesse would go through Gossip Central. Jesse trudged through Gossip Central thinking, *where is that girl and what's going on here*? Suddenly, there was a flash of lightning followed by a sharp clap of thunder that caused Jesse to duck. Just as he ducked, he thought he saw a flashlight in the same area where he and MJ had found Howie. He turned to look again and was struck on the head from behind, and the lights went out.

—2—

Unaware of what was happening to Jesse, MJ and Neiko were methodically working their way through the tent area checking everywhere for clues of any sort. Earlier, Neiko had found three cell phones and an iPad that were left behind. They would eventually be returned to their rightful owners after their contents were checked out. MJ continued on toward the rec hall. The storm finally passed and the clouds were giving way to a bright full moon. The only thing better than this, MJ thought, would be to find that girl alive and well. Still, there were too many unanswered questions. And then he thought of listening to Billy-Bob pontificate. One could only guess what to expect.

Billy-Bob was originally a deputy in a small town in one of the Carolinas named Bensenville, population 125, minus Billy-Bob, that is. His father, the honorable Lawrence B. Benson, was the circuit judge, fondly called "Let-them-go Larry," by the local law enforcement officers. Billy-Bob's mother Harriet, as luck would have it, was the mayor of Bensenville, and was often referred to as "hairbreadth Harry." She was given this name because of the off-the-wall decisions she would make without regard for the general consensus of the town. They were usually concocted in the local beauty salon and then put into effect when she left. It was believed that between the both of them—Larry and Harry—they probably couldn't give you the definition of truth and/or justice. Taking all this into consideration one could easily see how Billy-Bob worked his way up in the sheriff department's ranks to investigator. Billy-Bob could be a top-notch investigator when he concentrated on the matters at hand. His problem was he liked to showboat, like his mother, and when he did, the investigation usually turned to shit. His only saving grace was the deputies working with him, who were pretty sharp guys, and who somehow managed to keep things under control.

MJ went into the rec hall not knowing what to expect, only to find it almost completely empty. "Where is everyone?" he asked Katie as he looked around.

"Well, Billy-Bob has made a decision that the girl is not here and decided to focus the investigation on Sunny Brook, the campground next door," she said.

"Oh, that's great. Where's Jesse?" MJ asked.

"He hasn't come back yet. We thought he was with you and Neiko."

"Oh shit, we split up on the way back. He should be here by now. Call the security patrol and have them sweep Gossip Central," MJ shouted, as he ran out the door to join the search.

The bright moon helped a little as the security teams swept the area. It was tedious walking due to the previous rainstorm. Shadows danced in the headlight and flashlight beams as the men on foot sloshed and slipped, checking for any sign of Jesse.

Finally someone shouted, "Hey, over here! I found him in the trench."

Jesse was just coming around as Rick propped him up. "Looks like we need rescue here, he has a pretty good gash on the back of his head," he shouted.

Jesse pulled Rick close and whispered with a painful groan "no rescue, get MJ."

It was only seconds before MJ arrived. He looked at Jesse and said, "take him to Doc's camp as quick as you can. I'll call ahead."

They put Jesse in a security cart and Rick told the others to resume patrol while he and MJ brought Jesse to Doc's. By the time they arrived at Doc's camp, Jesse had regained full consciousness. He was covered with mud and blood and mad as hell at himself for being careless. One look at his head and Peachy said, "I think you need stitches—let's go to the clinic."

"No clinic. Can you put a butterfly on it?" Jesse asked. Peachy looked over at Doc and he gave her a nod. "Okay, but first you need to get cleaned up so I can see what I'm doing."

Doc looked at MJ and said, "Call Rescue and have them send an ambulance over here for transport."

Jesse told Rick to go back and supervise the search party and concentrate on the area where he was found. As Rick turned to leave, Doc said with a wink, "Rick, there's one more thing . . . Jesse is in bad shape and we're sending him to Mass. General in Boston tonight. The ambulance should arrive shortly. Send it here."

"Okay, Doc, got you covered," Rick said as he left.

"Wait a minute, I'm not going to Boston tonight or any other time," Jesse snarled.

"Relax, you're not going anywhere except to take a shower, so we can fix that cut. For the time being, you're staying here out of sight. Peachy will make the spare bed for you," Doc said.

MJ looked at Doc and nodded. Someone didn't like the way Jesse was snooping around. With him out of the picture for a while, maybe they would slip up.

After Jesse was cleaned up and his wound patched, the three of them sat down and began putting what they knew of the case together. "The only definite thing we have so far is a missing sixteen-year-old girl. Since we have pretty well eliminated the transients, it leaves us with the remaining permanent residents and the parents," Doc said.

"I think we should run a Triple I on the parents. There's something not right and we need all the help we can get," MJ said.

"I agree. Maybe you can use some of your clout through the governor to do that. We have no authority. And while you're at, it let's do one on our mister nice guy, Howard Wang. There's something about that guy that bugs the hell out of me," Jesse joined in.

Triple I stands for Interstate Investigation Index, which is used to identify anyone that has been arrested throughout the country. It's a valuable tool for police to use during investigations. It's similar to NCIC (National Crime Information Center), but is a little more in-depth.

"You know, I agree. I think we should find out all we can about the missing girl's deceased parents. There might be something useful there," Doc said.

"I'll get right on that first thing in the morning, and I better check with Billy-Bob in case he turned up something at the camp next door," MJ said.

MJ started out the door heading to the office for a final security check and some much needed rest. Jesse called after him, "Hey, MJ, keep your head down," to which they all had a good laugh.

The remainder of the night passed quietly, with a few false alarms. Two different patrols reported what they thought was an occasional flashlight beam, but by the time they got to the location, there was nothing. One patrol leader, a seasoned, crusty old security guard named Tom, said, "It's like someone's playing with us. Or it's a ghost."

"Perfect," MJ said. "Just what we need. A ghost. Okay guys let's start questioning the remaining residents. Be specific and take good notes."

Just as they were leaving, MJ overheard one man say to another, "Too bad about Jesse. How long do you think he'll be in Boston?" *Nice*, MJ thought. *Rick did his job exactly the way we wanted him to. The word is out.*

MJ made his way over to Doc's to fill them in on the night's developments. "Nothing new to report. Flashlights and ghosts top the list. The most important thing is, Rick did his job and planted the seed. Oh, and I have about twenty texts and emails for you, from all our friends in low places," he told Jesse.

"Like who? And what about?"

"The word is out, O Great One, that you have been injured. Let me read a few," MJ chuckled. "Here's one from Diamond Dave: *'Hey, need me to bring a light?'* You never give Dave a lighter unless you want a place burned—especially if he has a can of gas in his hand. Homeless Joe will attest to that, when he sobers up. It seems Diamond Dave had the wrong address one night and Homeless Joe paid the price. Then there's Hawkeye Jim: *'Jesse, I can pack my guns in an hour—he's dead—just call me—oh—don't give this number out, okay?'* And Wayne the guide: *'My friend, tell me who you want found—I got you covered.'* Then of course the Wookie, who looks and acts like a gorilla: *'Send me an address, I will rip off his head and use it for a bowling ball.'* And last but not least, don't forget Mr. Giggles, who thinks pushing people off bridges or into traffic is a fun sport: *'Jesse, just say the word—I'll be there. I have a new move to show you.'* I could go on and on."

This group of lunatics represents only a handful of Jesse's other-side-of-the-tracks acquaintances that he has dealt with in the past. "Boy, ya gotta love those guys—they're great backup if you need it," Jesse said with a big smile. "But please don't call them. We have enough problems."

—3—

Day 2 came and went without a trace of the girl or a solid clue to her whereabouts. All the permanent residents were checked and rechecked, with no luck at all. MJ was at the office checking on the progress of the Triple I when a resident came into the store. Katie spoke briefly with them, then turned to MJ. "Was Billy-Bob here last night?"

"No, he was down the street in that other campground doing interviews. Why?"

Katie appeared shaken, her face a little pale. "That resident wanted to know who the deputy was that she saw last night down by where Jesse was found."

MJ dropped his half-eaten donut on the floor. The hair on his arms stood up. "Oh shit! I have to go see Jesse and Doc," he said, as he ran out the door.

MJ informed Jesse and Doc about what had just transpired at the office. "Great," Jesse growled. "What did Tom the security guard say about a ghost? Just what we need, not that we don't have enough problems. What about the Triple I inquiry?"

"We discovered that Ken is still fighting the Vietnam war, at least in his head for a while—had a couple of DWIs, but has been clean since he went to work for the state about ten years ago. Barbie is clean as a whistle, they appear to be nice people. No response on the deceased parents as of yet. They said it would be a while."

"Dammit, can't you use some of the governor's clout to speed things up?" Jesse shouted.

"Okay, relax. I'll make a call," MJ replied.

"Sorry man, it's not you, it's me. I'm just frustrated there's a girl out there that needs to be found, and I mean soon! Instead of being out there looking for her, I'm in here hiding, and then I'm told we have a ghost helping us. That's just what we need. What about Howard? Anything on him?"

"A laundry list. That guy is a winner for sure. Get this—he's originally from Houlton, Maine, a town of about 6,000. It lies about twenty-five minutes north of Haynesville, Maine, at the end of I-95, near the Canadian border. He was described as a loner, by anyone that knew or knows him. He isn't known to socialize or go out of his way to be friendly. He was an EMT in the fire department, and that's about the only good thing anyone said about him. In the past he had several domestic assaults, one assault on a police officer, a couple of DWIs, and a peeping tom charge. Been married and divorced twice, then just fell off the radar until we inquired—obviously worth looking at," MJ answered. "I gotta go make some phone calls to the governor's office to try and speed things up with the Triple I." It was common knowledge that when Governor Brennan requested something done, everything else stopped until it was done.

After MJ left, Jesse wondered aloud. "What about the deputy! What about the ghost! What the hell is going on here?"

"I know!" Doc replied. "Tom the security guard has been here a long time. He's a no-nonsense kind of guy. I think he made the ghost comment out of frustration. Nevertheless, he did say he saw a flashlight beam several times last night that he couldn't explain. Then we have a resident reporting to Katie that he saw a deputy in the area where you were found. . . ."

"You know what I'm thinking . . ." Doc smiled.

"I certainly do, but I don't believe in this ghost bullshit for one minute, do you? Jesse asked.

"No more than you do, but you must admit, it's not the first time people say they have seen him," Doc sighed.

Doc was referring to their old friend and colleague David Burns, Katie's late husband, who suddenly passed away last year. David had been a sworn deputy sheriff and a member of the Blue Knights motorcycle organization—an international law enforcement motorcycle club. The club had been originally formed in Maine back in 1974 and spread nationwide. While he was alive, Katie and David ran the campground together like a well-oiled machine. David had a friendly way about him that was contagious. His "we-can-do-anything anytime" attitude, seemed to rub off on people, along with his "don't-try-me, if you don't like it my way" persona. David had two sides, and it was better to stay on his good side. Other campground owners and managers would come from all over the country to visit his campground to get ideas on how to run theirs more efficiently. After David's death, there were multiple reports of people seeing him here and there on the grounds, quite often in his deputy uniform. Others would report feeling his presence with no explanation. These sightings always seemed to happen when something was amiss at the campground. Almost like he was there, trying to help.

"I hear you, I just don't believe it. Dammit, I need a drink, my head hurts and what the hell's taking MJ so long?" Jesse groaned.

No sooner had the words left Jesse's mouth than MJ arrived with a folder full of papers. "Here it is bossman, the report on the deceased parents," MJ said.

"The late Peggy Sue and William J. Johnson, formerly of 845 Route 2, Haynesville, Maine. Haynesville is a small town in the northern part of the state, boasting a whopping population of 122 people."

The report indicated neither Peggy Sue nor William had any previous incidents with law enforcement. They were the go-to people of the town—friendly upstanding residents of Haynesville. Sue taught second grade at the elementary school and

Sunday school at their church. She was a member of the PTA and a member of the American Legion, along with her husband. They were both veterans of the Vietnam war. William was an auto mechanic at a local garage, which he had planned to purchase. Neighbors said he would do minor repairs on their cars at home on Sundays after church, and not charge them. He was also a little league coach in his spare time. William and Peggy Sue had one child, a daughter by the name of Susan. Both parents were killed in a motor vehicle accident, early one snowy September night, as they traveled home from a church function.

The accident happened on a stretch of road called the Haynesville woods, south of the town center. This particular piece of road was notorious for accidents, usually involving truckers. Before I-95 was completed, truckers would use Route 2, which ran through Haynesville, or Route 9. Route 9, was commonly referred to as "the airline." It was given that name because it was used by the Airline Stage Company years ago. It was their main route, when they were heading south to New Hampshire or Massachusetts. Route 2 also headed south and was heavily traveled. There's a stretch of Route 2 that goes through the Haynesville woods, which is full of curves and turns. This particular stretch was extremely slippery when it was wet or snow covered. Most of the locals avoided it after dark.

"Okay, what else have you got?" Jesse asked.

"It appears there were a few questions concerning the accident that have never been cleared up. The vehicle the Johnsons were driving in was broadsided by a van heading south. The part that's confusing is, the accident happened on a straight stretch of road. The question is, why broadside? There were no witnesses, and whoever was driving the van was never found. The original investigators had noted what appeared to be many footprints in the snow, indicating the possibility that several people may have been there. Unfortunately, no further follow-up was done, mainly because accidents in this area are so frequent." MJ paused, then continued his report.

"The only survivor of the crash was a young girl, the Johnson's daughter, who had been a passenger in the car. At the time of the accident, it was believed the girl was also killed. They had all but given up, when an alert EMT at the scene detected she had a pulse. The ambulance rushed her to the hospital, and after a lengthy stay she recovered. She seemed perfectly normal physically, except for a slight limp," MJ replied.

"Wonderful, a lot of good that does us. When you get a minute, put in a call to Squeaky and see if she can help those folks out when she gets a chance." Jesse said.

Squeaky, aka Marie Green, was a top-notch—if not the best—accident reconstructionist in the three-state area. She got the name Squeaky from those that knew her, because of the way she giggled when she found clues that dozens of investigators had missed. She was undoubtedly one of a kind.

"Okay, now back to our own case," Jesse grumbled.

"Oh but Great One, the girl that survived the accident walks with a limp. What do you think? Do we have some kind of connection here?"

"Holy shit," Jesse jumped out of his chair. "That could be the same girl we're looking for, but what in the hell does that accident have to do with her being missing now?"

"Hold on guys, there may be more to this than you think. I'm gonna make some calls. Stay here and make us a drink," Doc said.

MJ and Jesse sat and bounced all kinds of scenarios off each other, playing devil's advocate, hoping for an idea of some sort. "We have a missing girl, who at a younger age had been involved in a motor vehicle accident. Her parents were instantly killed at the time and it was assumed she was also dead at the scene. Fortunately, she survived but lay in a hospital for weeks. After her recovery and miles of bureaucratic paperwork, she was adopted by an upstanding family, hoping to live happily ever after," Jesse said.

"A few years go by and everything is fine and dandy. Then the family decides to go on a much-needed vacation and chooses Happy Valley. They pack up their belongings, come here to visit and the girl disappears. Why?"

"That's the 64 million dollar question," MJ replies.

* * *

The door popped open with a crash and Doc shouldered his way in with a huge stack of paperwork. He looked at Jesse and MJ and smiled. "Listen guys, my sources think we can find our answers here, if we look hard enough. And my sources are never wrong, know what I mean?"

The three of them began sorting and organizing papers, when Jesse's phone rang. He quickly answered it. "Great, just what we need. I'll tell the guys. Stay calm, Katie," and hung up. "Another sighting last night of flashlight beams in the field. What the hell's going on around here? It's like someone's looking for something, but what? Besides that, how are they avoiding the security patrol?"

"Maybe we could saturate the fields with our security," MJ replied.

"Trouble with that is the light beams are random, so how do we know when to make a move?"

"I think you're right! It's like we're dealing with a ghost who appears and disappears whenever it's convenient," MJ sputters.

"Ghost my ass. Someone knows our every move and is taking advantage of it. Let's play along a while longer and see what happens. Meanwhile, don't discuss things out in the open, keep it between us. I have a plan," said Doc.

MJ headed up to the office to see what Katie had to say about the latest flashlight report, and to try and calm her down. But Katie was fine—only a little upset, which could only be expected after all that had happened. She didn't need any more ghost talk.

MJ was leaving the office when the phone rang. "It's Squeaky Green for you," Katie said.

MJ took the phone. "What have you got for me, Squeak?"

"Well," she said with her trademark giggle, you may be interested to know this accident shouldn't have happened. It could have and should have been avoided. I would venture a guess, not official yet, that someone was not paying attention, either impaired, or caused it to happen."

"Thanks, Squeaky," he said, and headed back to Doc's to let Doc and Jesse know what he had just learned from Squeaky.

* * *

"I had a suspicion about this whole mess," Doc said. "Now maybe we can make some sense out of this paperwork."

"You know, Doc, the girl's background comes into play somewhere, but shouldn't we concentrate on what's happening here first?" Jesse asked.

"I guess you're right. I have an idea that may help," Doc replied. "Let's put Neiko to work in the field and see if he comes up with anything. We might find whatever our flashlight searcher is looking for."

The campground, even with all its permanent campers, had several acres of neatly trimmed lawn blended nicely between and around each camp. Needless to say, this could be like finding a needle in a haystack, even for Neiko. "Why don't we go out just after dark? Neiko doesn't care and maybe our friend with the flashlight will appear," MJ said.

"Good idea," Doc said. "Jesse, you stay put. Remember you're still in a Boston hospital."

Just after dark, Doc, MJ, and Neiko headed out, not knowing

what to expect, hoping for the best. "Let's head to where Jesse was whacked," Doc said.

"This is as good a place to start as any. The light has been seen here also." After about twenty minutes of crisscrossing the area, Neiko sniffed out a digital watch and then a cell phone. "Alright Neiko, good boy. Let's go home," said MJ.

The trio headed back to Doc's place to see what information they could retrieve from the phone, and find out who the owner was. The watch owner could be a little harder to identify, unless it belonged to the same person, that is. One could only hope.

Back at Doc's, Jesse was elated when he saw what they had found. "Let's check it out. This could be the key. And this hiding shit is over now. I'm out of the hospital and back at camp. Spread the word."

"Got you covered, Jesse," MJ said. "I'll tell Rick—he knows what to do. He's one of us."

After a short while Jesse found what he was looking for in the phone. He dialed up the number and waited for someone to answer. All at once he made a face, then threw the phone on the sofa in disgust.

"What's wrong?" Doc asked.

"The damn phone belongs to that pain in the ass reporter, Windy Chase, from WHEIDI TV station in Goffstown, New Hampshire," Jesse said. "She came here to do a story on Neiko the day the girl went missing. So instead of going back to Milly's Tavern in Manchester and getting a snoot full, she stuck her snoot where it doesn't belong. She went out in the field here when she saw the light that night. She must have slipped or fell and dropped her phone. Her mother should have named her hemorrhoids instead of Windy, because she's a pain in the ass."

"Okay, guys calm down," MJ said. "I'll go out again with Neiko. We'll find what we want."

MJ was taking his time running things over in his mind.

Halfway back to the office, he stopped for a minute looking out into the darkness, his mind wandering. All at once he thought he heard a scraping sound, like something being moved. He waited a minute, shook his head and started to walk again. Then he saw it—a flashlight beam out in the field. *Holy shit*, he said to himself. "Let's go Neiko," he said quietly, and started running toward it. As quickly as it appeared, the light went out and all was quiet. MJ and Neiko continued on with caution, not wanting to get whacked like Jesse. About fifteen feet from where they found the first phone, and just about where they saw the light, Neiko stopped and indicated he smelled something. "Show me," MJ said to Neiko as he took out his flashlight. Neiko nosed a piece of sod that had been freshly turned over, revealing another phone lying in the mud. *Yes*, MJ said to himself. He whispered, "Come on Neiko, let's get the guys."

* * *

Back at Doc's all the lights were out and it was quiet. MJ banged on the door, "Open up guys! Take a look at this!" he yelled.

"We're right here," Doc said calmly. "Quiet down." He and Jesse were sitting on the porch having a drink.

"Look at this," MJ said, as he showed them the phone.

"Did you touch it with your hands?" Jesse asked.

"No, I had gloves on," MJ replied. "I didn't want to take any chances, hoping for prints."

"Good thinking," Jesse said. He put on a pair of gloves himself, then took the phone and turned it on. "Bingo! This is Sue Jones's phone—she's here. I knew it dammit, now we just have to find *her*. Please God let her be alive," he sighed.

"It's getting late, but we need to have another talk with the girl's parents. I'm assuming they're still here, correct Jesse?"

"Yes, they are, Doc. They're at the office with Katie and two security guards. I'll give Katie a heads up that we're coming and make sure the parents are there waiting for us."

"Let's go!" Jesse, Doc, and MJ headed to the office to see if they could get any more information from Sue's parents.

* * *

When they arrived, Jesse greeted Barbie and Ken and their daughter Lilly, who were anxiously waiting to hear what he had to say. He told them Sue's phone had been found on the grounds, and then began his inquiry.

"Listen folks, we are doing our best to locate your daughter, but we need a few more facts about her. Tell us what she's like, what she likes to do, who her friends are. We need details. What exactly does Sue do with her time?"

"She has always been very quiet, even before we adopted her," Barbie related. "The agency she was with had tried to bring her out of her shell to no avail. When she came to us, she began progressing slowly and is 90 percent better than she was. She used to just sit and stare out the window like she was in a trance. She hardly ever talked to anyone. Then one day, a classmate of hers came over and was doodling and sketching pictures. Sue got interested and started doing it herself. Now she's almost obsessed. It's good and it's bad, I guess. She's still very quiet, and now and then seems lost or daydreaming. But she's so much better than before,"

"Okay," Jesse said. "What were the sketches of—animals, trees, landscapes, or what?"

"Actually, they are mostly of people."

"Do you have any of them around that we can look at?" MJ asked.

"I'm not sure, she usually keeps them in her backpack, like they're a secret or something. She doesn't talk about them, so we don't push her," Barbie replied.

"Mom, I saw her drawing the other day. It looked like she

was drawing some people and some kind of car. She was crying a little. When I asked her if she was alright she stuffed the drawing in her bag and ran to the bathhouse," Lilly chimed in.

"See if you can find any of them," MJ said. "It's important."

"But I—" Barbie stammered.

"Right now lady, get them, I'm not asking, I'm telling you. Go look right now," MJ yelled as he slammed his hand on the table. After about fifteen minutes Barbie returned with a folder full of wrinkled hand-drawn sketches. She laid them in front of Jesse, Doc, and MJ.

"Let's see what we got," Jesse said. The trio sorted through the sketches and almost in unison said, "Oh boy."

Jesse turned to Barbie and Ken, "Looks like the sketches might be significant. Thank you for cooperating. We will handle it from here. You can go back to your camp for the time being." The three men waited until Barbie, Ken, and Lilly had left the office, and then continued their conversation.

"I think we opened a can of worms here," MJ said, as they looked at each other.

"I'm not sure what you guys think, but I have to make a call. I'll go outside—it's private. Hang on for a minute," Doc said. Upon his return, Doc motioned for Jesse and MJ to come with him, and as they left the office for Doc's place, he said, "I have someone coming to help us out. I'll explain over a drink, unless you guys don't want one, that is."

"Very funny," MJ said.

* * *

Back at his camp, Doc poured a tall drink for each of them. "Unless my mind is imagining things, Sue was drawing pictures of the accident she was in. That would account for the car in the sketch, and the stick figures must represent people that were involved. What do you guys think?" Doc asked.

"No question in our minds. MJ and I were discussing the same thing while you were on the phone," Jesse said.

"Okay, it's agreed. We may have something big here—maybe even bigger than we think. I made a call to an acquaintance of mine who will be joining us by tomorrow to help us out. He's currently working undercover in Toledo, Ohio, at a VA center. Let me warn you of something ahead of time. This guy is a little scary, so be careful what you say to him unless I'm around. He's a former Delta Force counter intelligence operative who works alone. Most of his time is spent undercover, behind enemy lines. They call him Choo-Choo-Charlie. They gave him that name years ago as a joke. He was orphaned at a young age and grew up alone. He lived in a shack next to the railroad yard with no supervision or guidance, except what little he'd get from train crews. They kind of adopted him and tried to keep him straight and alive. I must admit they did a pretty good job. He grew up tough, mean, and was street savvy at a very young age. He's always been obsessed with trains—that's how he got the nickname. You have no reason to know his real name. He's crazy as a shithouse mouse, speaks six languages fluently, and is deadly. His idea of fun is ripping off people's ears or cutting their throats.

"I called him because among his many talents, he is an expert sketch analyst. He can see a sketch and if the person in the sketch has been in our radar, he will identify him or her without question. If the people aren't identifiable, he takes different parts of the sketch and tries to make sense of it. People I know all around the world use him when they need an expert, and he's yet to be wrong. At least that's what I've been told. Of course, it could be that no one had the nerve to tell him if he was. He, my friends, is gonna tell us who's in the sketch. At the least he'll tell us what the sketch is trying to signify. All we can do is wait and see." Doc said with a smile. "It's time for us to wrap this show up. We will saturate this place tomorrow. MJ, have Rick gather our most trusted security guards and meet us at the rec hall at six a.m. Let's call it a night. We have about two hours before we start all this up again."

—4—

Morning arrived with bright sun and a cloudless blue sky. The search team was assembled in the rec hall drinking coffee and waiting for instructions. Jesse, Doc, and MJ had arrived ahead of the group so they could set up a search plan that would coordinate teams, designate team leaders, issue radios, and give instructions.

Jesse leaned over to Doc and said, "Billy-Bob can't help us out. It just happens that the high profile residents from the you-know-what compound are going to be in town. Looks like Billy-Bob wants his name in the paper, so he'll be tied up all weekend."

"That's okay. He's an idiot anyway. We can handle it. If this is what I'm beginning to think it is, I have an ace in the hole."

"Listen, guys," Jesse said to the group. "This has to be the most thorough search effort you have ever performed. There's a teenage girl out there somewhere. We don't know if she's lost, injured, or being held against her will. Don't leave a stone unturned, check behind every rock and stump you encounter. Remember, this girl's life could depend on each of you. As each team finishes their sector, come back here and get refreshed. We will then assign you another sector until the camp has been completely crossed and crisscrossed in every direction. Anything comes up, team leaders, let us know right away. That's it guys, good luck."

After all the teams had left, MJ turned to Doc and asked, "When is your ace in the hole arriving, do you have any idea?"

"He already did," Doc said. "He was that little guy with the beard serving coffee to the teams."

"Are you kidding? That little guy?"

"I don't kid when we have a situation like this," Doc replied. "That was our man."

"Where is he now?" MJ asked.

"He's gone. Who knows?" Doc said. "When he's ready to talk we'll know. I showed him the sketches early this morning before you arrived. He said there wasn't much to work with, but he'd do his best. Actually, he's on it already. Remember what I told you about this guy, so relax—you never poke the bear."

* * *

As the day went on, the search crews would come in, get a coffee and sandwich then be sent back out to another sector. Just a little after six p.m., the last crew returned, and like the others had found nothing.

Jesse thanked them all for their effort and told them to get some dinner and rest and return in the morning at six a.m.

"Where in hell can she be?" Jesse asked Doc and MJ. "There's not an inch of this place that we haven't searched and researched. I don't get."

"That's the key word my friend, research," a voice from the shadows in the back of the hall calls out. "How about checking to see if there's been any new construction done here on the grounds lately. Something that's not obvious, and you had to be involved to know about it. Let me know what you find out. Just tell Doc, he'll know where to find me." Then the back door opened and closed.

"That was only Charlie," Doc said with a smile. "Let's go have a talk with Katie."

When they arrived at the office, the trio found Katie sitting at her desk surrounded by folders and folders of paperwork.

"Busy, Katie?" Jesse asked with a grin.

"Just a little," she said, a tired smile on her face. "It never ends, you know. The season ends, but the new one begins at the same time. Sometimes it's a little chaotic, but if you're gonna play the game you have to play it right—take the good with the bad and make it better next year. But besides that, what can I do for my three wise men? How about we start with a drink—you guys look like and I feel like we all need one."

"Sounds good Katie, you're a woman after my own heart," Jesse said.

The four of them sat around the office discussing all the repairs and renovations that had been done in the past year. Nothing seemed unusual and all areas identified had been checked. "

"What about upgrades in the camp itself?" Doc asked.

"We did upgrade our water service and drainage system. What a mess that turned out to be," Katie said.

"What do you mean by that, Katie?" Jesse asked.

"We ran miles of water lines without any problem, but the drainage was another story. The rains came in and lasted a couple of weeks, flooding part of Gossip Valley, and we had pumps running 24/7 trying to get the pipes in the mud. We finally made a diversion trench, sort of a French Drain, and had to block that entire area off completely from our residents and campers. It seemed to have worked for us, but I don't really know what they did over there."

"Who does—someone had to have a plan and oversee what was going on?" MJ asked.

"David was in charge of course," she said with a sigh.

"It's okay, Katie," Jesse said. "We understand. Take your time."

After a moment Katie said, "He never did finish it. We had an outside contractor come in for that."

"Do you have the name of the contractor? We can give him a call and get the details," Doc said.

"Actually, I don't," Katie answered. "Howie volunteered to get that portion of the drain completed, to save me from worrying about it. He knew some contractor that was available, and within a day trucks and equipment were here working. Howie has been such a big help around here."

"Glad to hear that," Jesse said. "I think we have to have a talk with him and see what information he may have for us."

"He's not here right now," Katie said. "He went up north to Houlton to take care of some personal business. He expected to be gone a couple of days."

"Okay," Doc said. "Can you show us on the map where the work has been done? In the morning we will look around and see if it could have a bearing on the case."

"Sure," Katie replied. "I can show you the area on the camp map anyway. It may not be exact but it's in the area."

"That will work," Jesse said. "We can go from there."

Before sending the search crews out, Jesse briefed them on the latest developments, gave them instructions on what he wanted, and sent them out. As the crews were leaving, he called Rick aside and asked him to come with them.

Doc, MJ, Jesse, and Rick proceeded to the area Katie had indicated on the map as the place the construction had taken place.

"Okay, guys," Jesse said. "Let's locate all the drain pipes in this area, then we'll check them out."

"I remember when they did this work," Rick said. "They wouldn't let us down here for safety's sake. There must be a bunch of pipes. It took long enough for them to finish it."

After about three hours of wading through the weeds, bushes, and overgrowth they completed their search. The final outcome resulted in finding three large pipes protruding slightly out of the embankment.

"Well, Doc," Jesse said, "What do you think—now the fun part?"

"Yeah," Doc said. "I hate this part. You never know what's living in these damn things, but we have no choice. I hope there's no snakes."

"We'll send Rick in first," Jesse said with a smile. "He's not afraid of snakes."

"Hell I'm not," Rick said, and they all laughed.

"Okay, guys, which one first?" MJ asked. "Let's get it over with."

"Hey, did you notice that the one on the far end was really grown over? Almost like it wasn't working that well or blocked? Rick asked. "It also appears a little higher on the bank than the others."

"You're right," Jesse said. "Even though all three are grown over, you can see where the water has been running. On the first two the gravel is all loose and sandy on the last one nothing."

"What do you say we try that one first?" Doc asked.

The four men worked their way up the embankment the best they could, until they reached the pipe. MJ was the first one to get to it and yelled back, "Holy shit, this pipe is so huge you can crawl inside it."

"Watch yourself," Jesse said. "You never know what to expect."

"Let's find out," MJ chuckled, took out his flashlight, and crawled inside. A few minutes went by and finally MJ emerged from the pipe with a strange look on his face.

"Guys," he said, "you gotta see this yourself. That pipe goes in about four feet then steps down and there's a door. I opened it, and it's a bunker about ten feet square with a table, chairs, a cot, and a few sealed boxes."

"Just what I thought," Doc said. "That rotten bastard. He'll get his if it's the last thing I do."

In the time that Jesse had known Doc, he had never seen him so annoyed. "What is it, Doc," he asked.

"Start putting two and two together," he replied. "You'll figure it out. First things first, we have a teenage girl to find. Let's leave this place like we found it. Straighten the bushes out front as you leave so it looks like nobody's been here."

The day was drawing to an end. The search crews had returned and were released by their team leaders. Jesse, Doc, MJ, and Rick made their way back to the office to regroup their thoughts and have a stiff drink.

"What have we missed or overlooked?" MJ asked with a dejected tone. "Dammit I'm mad! Where is she?"

When they arrived at the office, Katie met them at the door. "I'm going to do my evening drive," she said. Katie always did an early morning and an evening drive through the campground, making sure things were okay. "By the way, when I get back, if you guys are mixing," she continued, "make mine a double. It's been one of those days."

"While you're mixing," Doc said to Jesse, "I have to make a quick call."

When Doc returned, the four of them sat around the table recounting all of their previous efforts to find Susan. Each of them shaking their heads and staring off as they asked and answered each question posed by the other. They kept getting the same results each time a question was asked. We did that or we tried that, appeared to be the common answer.

Suddenly the front door swung open and Katie was standing there with a startled look on her face. "Hey guys, I was just parking the car and I swear I heard something in the rear basement room. I went to look but there's no light back there and I couldn't see anything. I called out but got no response so when I came out, I locked all the doors from the outside. If someone is in there, they can't get out. Maybe that prowler that was looking into campers a few weeks ago is back."

"Let's take a look," Jesse said. "Katie, I want you to stay here. MJ, bring Neiko. If someone's hiding down there they may have some electronics on them and he can sniff them out."

The four of them went to the basement and entered through a small walk-in door, leaving the larger doors locked. "Rick, you guard the door, the rest of us will begin a sweep," Jesse said. "Turn on every light in the place, let's put visibility on our side."

The trio started methodically searching the different sections of the basement. Searching a building or a room is not as easy as one would think. It's tedious and time consuming. One of the first things to do is turn on as many lights as possible. Then go room by room listening and looking everywhere. Check behind doors, under tables and beds, check for trap doors in the floor and ceiling, even behind heavy drapes. Once you're sure there is no one there, you call out to the other searchers which room is clear and move on to the next room. This is what the trio of investigators did until they were satisfied the building was clear.

"Okay, it doesn't look like there's anybody here," Jesse said. "You and Neiko want to give it a try, MJ?"

"You bet," MJ replied. "Let me get Neiko. Why don't you guys stand by for a minute in case something moves."

MJ put Neiko through his usual routine walking around, letting him smell, watching to see if he sensed anything. After they had checked the area from one end to the other, MJ put Neiko's work collar on and told him, "let's work." They went back and forth around the room with MJ directing Neiko, telling him to search, seek, over and over again.

Just as they were finishing up the last section Neiko stopped, and indicated he smelled something. "Show me," MJ said, and Neiko nosed a broken board in the wall. Again MJ said, "show me" and Neiko again nosed the board hard. MJ stepped back and pulled on the broken board as hard as he could. The board was actually a makeshift door that gave way when he pulled it. Just inside the opening, MJ saw what Neiko smelled. It was the faint glow of an iPad lying on the concrete floor. In the far corner of the room there was movement in the shadows.

"Is someone there?" MJ asked. In return he heard what sounded like a small whimper. "Don't be afraid," he said softly, "I'm a policeman. This is my dog Neiko. Who are you?"

"I'm Susan," a little voice sobbed.

"Hi Susan, everything's going to be okay," MJ said. "Can Neiko visit you?"

"I guess," she whispered.

"Neiko, go visit," MJ said. The little girl knelt down and began hugging Neiko and crying openly.

MJ turned around and said, "We found her, guys, it's Susan. She appears okay. Let's give her a minute with Neiko."

"Thank God," Jesse said to himself. He then turned and called to Rick, who was still guarding the door, "Go get Katie and bring her down here. We found Susan."

Katie arrived in less than a minute. "Where is she, Jesse?" she asked.

"In the far back room," Jesse answered, "with MJ and Neiko. We didn't want to scare her, so we thought you could talk to her for a few minutes."

"You bet," Katie replied, "I'll go back there." Katie walked up to the door of the faintly lit room and saw Susan kneeling with her arms around Neiko.

"Hi Susan, remember me? I'm Katie from the office."

Susan shook her head and tearfully said, "yes."

"Well everything's going to be alright. Let's get out of here and find you something to eat." She placed a small blanket she had been carrying over Susan's shoulders and put her arm around her. Susan, who was still holding tightly onto Neiko, looked at Katie.

Katie smiled and said, "Don't worry, he's coming with us," and she guided Susan, with Neiko by her side, through the garage back to the office.

After they left, Jesse, Doc, and MJ went into the area Susan had been hiding to look around for any further evidence or information she may have left behind. All they found were the iPad on the floor and her backpack, full of cookies, juice drinks, and candy wrappers, in the corner. They took these items with them and went back upstairs to the rec room.

"Okay, guys," Jesse said, "let's give her a little time with Katie. In the meantime Rick, go get the parents, Ken and Barbie, and bring them here. MJ, call Billy-Bob and tell him we found her safe and sound here on the property, and he can come by anytime he's available. When you guys finish, let's all meet back here in the rec room. After Susan's calmed down and had a little time with her parents we'll try to get to the bottom of this."

* * *

Just as MJ hung up the phone with Billy-Bob, Ken and Barbie and Lilly came rushing through the door with tears in their eyes and smiles on their faces. "She's out in the office with Katie, folks, go right in," Jesse said.

Just as Ken and Barbie went into the office, Rick came in the door looking puzzled. "What's wrong, Rick?" Doc asked. "You look like you saw a ghost."

"When I went to get Ken and Barbie they were already on their way here," Rick replied. "They told me they knew something must have happened, when they saw the deputy."

"What deputy?" Doc asked. "There's no deputies here."

"Well," Rick said, "they claimed to have seen a deputy out in the field looking around, he clapped his hands together and walked down the fence line." The silence in the room was deafening. They all just looked at each other.

Finally, Jesse said, "Okay MJ, did you talk to Billy-Bob?"

"Yes I did," he chuckled. "Billy-Bob says there's no reason for him to come out here unless you really need him."

"What?" Jesse stammered, "call that fat hillbilly back and tell him to get his lazy ass out here. This is an open missing persons case. That girl was reported missing three days ago and has now been located. It's his responsibility to verify she's been found and close the damn case."

"Okay, I'm on it," MJ chuckled. "This should be fun."

"It's time we start putting things together guys," Jesse said. "By the way, Doc, what happened to your invited helper? Did he quit on us?"

"Actually" Doc replied, "he's been pretty busy. He was with Squeaky Green, up in Haynesville yesterday, going over some material he wanted to verify. Remember I told you in the beginning, he comes and goes as he pleases until he gets results. That call I made earlier was to bring him up to speed with what we had found at the drains. He didn't seem a bit surprised. He asked us to find out if Susan had any more sketches in her backpack. He wants to see them."

"Okay, Doc, just checking. I want to get all our ducks in a row," Jesse replied. "Let's go see if Susan has calmed down enough to talk to us."

Just as Jesse was about to open the door to the office and talk to Susan, the rec room's rear door burst open and Billy-Bob walked in.

"Hold it right there, McGrath," he yelled. "I don't know where you're going but I want to make one thing clear. I've had just about all the cheap shit I'm going to take from you. Since you insist on telling me how to do my job, I intend to do it. Right now I'm considering arresting you and your group of vigilantes for interfering and impeding a police investigation. I might also charge one of you with impersonating a police officer. So sit your ass down over there with the rest of your people, while I speak with the girl. If you have a problem with that, my deputies will be glad to hook you up right now. What's it going to be?"

"You're in charge, Billy-Bob," Jesse said. "We don't want any problem."

"You bet you don't," Billy-Bob said. "Where's the girl?"

"She's in the office with Katie," Jesse replied. "Go right in."

Billy-Bob went into the office to speak with Susan and her parents and closed the door behind him. Seconds later the door reopened and Katie came out.

"He said I wasn't needed," she smiled. After a little more than an hour, Billy-Bob came out with a big smile on his face.

"Okay, chief of security, I'm finished here," he snickered. "As far as I'm concerned, this was just a family problem. The girl was rebelling against her parents and she went into hiding to teach them a lesson. I'm closing this case down officially as of now, and will report my findings as necessary. Next time you want to play boy scout, find a different county, or I'll have your ass." With that being said, Billy-Bob turned, with a big smile on his face and headed for the door.

Just then, Doc called out, "Hey, deputy can we have a word?"

"Sure," Billy-Bob answered. "Who are you, the assistant scout leader?"

"Let me introduce myself," Doc said as he handed him a business card. Billy-Bob looked at the card and then at Doc. Doc put his arm on Billy-Bob's shoulder like they were old friends, as they walked toward the door. Doc was talking too softly to be heard by anyone but Billy-Bob, who was nodding his head in acknowledgment, as he closed the door.

"What was that all about?" Jesse asked.

"Well," Doc replied with a chuckle. "I thanked him for doing such a good job with closing the case. Then I told him my people would be in the area on a different matter and would not need his help. Oh yeah, I forgot to mention. I told him to keep his wise ass hillbilly nose out of it, or I'd have him pushing shopping carts for WalMart on the Canadian border."

"Okay, now that we've gotten over that hurdle," Jesse said, "let's see if we can find out what's going on with Susan."

"Wait a second what about this," Rick said, as he held up the backpack he had picked up downstairs.

"Damn," MJ said. "We forgot all about it—where was it?"

"I sat on it when Billy-Bob came in," Rick smiled, "so he wouldn't see it and think we had something."

"Perfect," Doc said. "Let's see what's inside before we talk to Susan."

They opened the pack and dumped the contents on the table. There were pencils, pens, socks, underwear, some candy bars, a small flashlight, and a large writing pad. When they picked up the writing pad, a small photo fell out.

"Look at this," Jesse said. "It's Susan, and that must be her mom and dad." They started turning the pages in the writing pad and found sketches of what appeared to be a man. There were also sketches of several other figures and some kind of truck or van.

"Oh boy," Doc said. "Do you realize what we might have here? Let me have the clearest sketch. You guys go talk to Susan. I have to call Charlie right now."

"Okay boys and girls, let's go see Susan," Jesse said, as he opened the office door. When they entered the office they saw Susan sitting on the floor with Neiko's head in her lap. "Hi again, Susan," MJ said, "I'm the policeman you talked with downstairs, remember?"

"Hi MJ," Susan said without hesitation. "Yes I do, thank you for letting Neiko visit me."

"He can visit anytime we're around," he told her. "Tell me Susan, why were you hiding? Did something frighten you?"

Susan stopped smiling and just stared out the window, as tears formed in her eyes. She slowly nodded her head yes, sobbed and buried her face in Neiko's fur.

"That's okay, Susan," MJ said. "You don't have to be afraid anymore, we won't let anything happen to you. These are my friends, Jesse and Rick—we are all here to help you. We know it's hard, but try not to be too nervous. We just need you to answer a few more questions, okay?"

"Yes," she said softly.

"Has it got something to do with these sketches?" Jesse asked, as he held one up.

She nodded her head yes and said, "It's him."

"What about him?" MJ asked. "Who is he?"

"He was there," she sobbed."

"He was where, Susan?" Jesse asked. "Where was he?"

Susan continued sobbing but finally said, "I saw him at the accident."

"You mean the one where you got injured, Susan?" She nodded her head yes again. "That's all in the past Susan, he's gone away somewhere, and can't hurt you anymore," MJ said.

"No, he's not," she wailed. "He's here—I saw him."

"You saw him here in the campground?" Jesse asked. "Is that why you ran and hid?"

"Yes," she sobbed.

"Did you tell your mom and dad that you saw him?" Jesse asked.

"No, I was too scared. I don't want them to get hurt."

"Well, don't worry any more Susan, we are going to find him if he's still here. Nobody's going to get hurt, okay?"

"Okay," she murmured.

"Ken, you and Barbie go to your camp and get enough things to last you all a few days," Jesse said. "You're all staying here at the office with Katie and Rick for the time being. There will also be a security patrol keeping watch from an unknown location."

"Is this all necessary?" Barbie asked.

"I don't know," Jesse responded. "Just a precautionary adjustment. Better safe than sorry. Right, MJ?"

"Right," MJ said. "We can't be too careful."

Jesse called Rick aside and said, "You know what to do. No one in or out of this place except us. No one knows we found Susan. I'm not going to tell the security patrol—we don't know who to trust. I'll get Tom the security guard and have him hidden on the outside, I know we can trust him, and he's reliable. In the meantime we have to find Doc and fill him in." As he started to leave, Jesse reached inside his jacket, turned his back, so no one could see, and slipped Rick his Smith and Wesson forty caliber duty pistol. "Just in case," he whispered. "I've seen you use one of these many times if you recall, he said with a sad smile."

"Not to worry, I have mine with me," Rick replied.

* * *

The campground was quiet as Jesse and MJ headed to Doc's place. Doc had left to contact Charlie earlier and hadn't returned. Knowing Doc, they assumed he was home at his place having a drink. Both men remained silent as they walked, tossing all the events of the day back and forth in their head hoping to make sense of them. They wanted to advise Doc of their interview with Susan. They also wanted him to know about moving the family into the office with security guarding them. All at once, MJ tapped Jesse on the arm and whispered, "Look, in the field, do you see it?"

"Holy shit," Jesse whispered back. "Let's go slow and quiet so we don't spook him or her." The pair moved into the field, trying to keep the light in view without revealing themselves.

"Careful, it's moving toward the drainage ditches," MJ whispered. "Wait, it disappeared—where did it go—am I losing it?"

"Hold on, I think I know what's going on now," Jesse said. "Let's go see the Doc."

They arrived at Doc's place just as he was sitting down on his porch with a tall drink. "Hey guys, ready for one?"

"Be serious," MJ said. "After a night like this, who isn't?" Jesse and MJ filled Doc in on all the events of the day.

"What do you think, Doc?" Jesse asked.

"Well I must admit I was pretty sure what this was all about from the beginning, but now, from what you just told me, I'm almost positive. I would have told you guys earlier but I had to be sure. That's why I gave Charlie the sketches and sent him up north. Let's see if he comes up with a little more definite information. So what are your thoughts on the flashlight?"

"Well, I've been giving this whole flashlight thing some serious thought," Jesse started. "We keep getting these sightings at different times and places. At first I was sure there was a definite reason for them, but now I think I have it figured out. Although the lights appear randomly, I've noticed they always seem to disappear in the same location. It happened again tonight. It disappeared down by the fence line that runs down the campground, just across the street from Sunny Brook. I think in the morning we should have a talk with our buddy, Billy Murphy, the campground engineer. He does all the repair work for both of these campgrounds and there isn't much he doesn't know. I'll tell him what I think, and see what he comes up with. If I'm right, our flashlight person comes from next door. He or she enters and exits through the fence, at the lower part of the campground, just before Gossip Valley. If you remember, MJ thought he heard a scraping noise just before he saw the light a few days ago. Well, there just happens to be a sliding metal panel installed on the fence in that area. It was put there years ago to allow access to the stream."

"Sounds like a plan," Doc said. "I think you're onto something that could also answer a few other questions."

"Okay," Jesse said. "Let's devise a plan to trap him or her — one that doesn't put anyone in danger."

"Everyone is in danger," Doc answered, "this guy doesn't want to be identified, nevermind caught. That accident took the lives of two people and he almost got away with it. But now my friends, we have a witness. I do agree with you that we need a plan. Let's call it a night, meet here in the morning and work something out."

—5—

Morning came bringing bright sunshine and cooler air, another perfect day in Happy Valley. Jesse and MJ made it a priority to call first thing on Billy Murphy, the campground engineer, and tell him what they thought.

"That wouldn't surprise me one bit," Billy said. "There's a lot of young punks staying there with time on their hands. You know it's not the best campground around, but I do have a few reliable sources over there. Let me ask around. Where can I find you guys if I get any information?"

"We'll be over at Doc's place if you come up with anything," Jesse answered.

Everyone in the area knew Billy. He was well-liked and respected. He was not the kind of guy you gave a hard time to. If he told you to move along, it would be in your best interest to do so, and if he asked a question, you'd better answer it.

The cool morning had given way to some warm sunshine, as the two investigators made their way to Doc's place. Just as they rounded the corner by the office they saw someone coming down the stairs.

"Hi, guys, good to see you," Howie said with a big smile. "I knew you guys would be busy closing down, so I hurried back from up north to give you a hand. Is everything okay? I went up to the office to tell Katie I was here, but it's locked up and the lights are out."

"Hi, Howie," Jesse said. "Everything's fine—glad you're back. We certainly need all the help we can get. Katie had to go to her sister's for some family matter. She should be back later. We had her lock everything up because there was no one to watch the store. We're too busy out here. You know how it is, you've done it enough."

"That's for sure," Howie responded with a grin. "Many, many times. I'm not fussy, what do you want me to do?"

"Well, fortunately we have most of the top side complete," Jesse replied. There is one big thing left and it's not a fun job, if you want. We need someone to check the lower fence line and drains, you never know what winter is going to throw our way."

"I'll be glad to do whatever needs to be done, Jesse," Howie said, "I've done it before."

"I know you have Howie, thanks," Jesse replied.

Jesse and MJ continued on their way to Doc's place. "Do you think he bought the Katie thing?" MJ asked.

"I think so," Jesse answered. "We can only hope—that snoopy bastard."

Just as they approached Doc's driveway, Billy Murphy came racing up in his work truck. He jumped out, went to the passenger's side of the truck and pulled open the door. "Come on you," he growled, as he reached in and pulled a long-haired teenager out by his ear. He dragged the boy over to Jesse and MJ. "Here's your flashlight shiner, Jesse. Tell them what you told me, Richie," Billy snarled.

The boy, Richie Long, a permanent resident at Sunny Brook, looked at Jesse and said, "Sorry."

"Sorry about what Jesse asked?"

"I'm the one that was shining the flashlight in the field every few days," Richie said.

"Why in the hell were you doing that?" MJ asked.

"The guy that works there said he was going to be away for a few days and he'd give me five dollars every time I went out," Richie answered. "He told me just shine the light around and then go out the fence line gate. He warned me if I got caught, I was on my own, and he wouldn't pay me. He said it was just a joke he was playing on you guys."

"What guy are you talking about?" Jesse asked.

"The little guy with the beard," Richie said. "They call him Howie, I think."

"Okay, Richie, you can go. If I find you or any of your friends on this property again I'll have you arrested, understand? Oh, by the way, you might want to have that ear looked at," Jesse said with a chuckle. "Thanks, Billy. Talk to you later."

"Well, what do you think of that," Jesse said to MJ. "Our friend Howie again. Case solved—let's tell Doc the latest."

* * *

"Hi guys," Doc greeted them. "Looks like Billy had some news for you out there."

"He sure did," Jesse smiled, "and you won't believe it. It seems like our flashlight idea was correct for one thing. The Long kid from next door was the light flasher, and guess who put him up to it?"

"You got me there my friend," Doc said. "Pray tell."

"Our friend Howie was paying him five dollars every time he did the light show. What do you make of that?" Jesse said.

"Well, I'll be damned," Doc said with a grin. "What else do you suppose that little rascal has been up to that we don't know about? Where is he now? Has he returned from his trip up north?"

"As a matter of fact, he returned a while ago," Jesse answered. "We have him checking the fence line and storm drains in Gossip Valley."

"That should be interesting," Doc replied, "especially after what we found there. I still haven't been able to figure what that's all about yet."

"Neither have we," MJ said, shaking his head. "There's gotta be a reason for it that we don't see. Well, I guess our next move is to confront him. At least about the flashlight thing."

"You're right MJ, maybe he'll tell us why he built the bunker at the same time," Jesse chimed in. "Let's head to the office parking area and wait for him to come back."

When the trio arrived at the parking area, they were surprised to see Rick standing outside the office door. He motioned for them to come inside. Once inside the office, they saw Susan sitting on the floor in the corner hugging Neiko and crying. Katie, Barbie, and Ken were kneeling in front of her talking softly, trying to console her.

"What the hell happened, Rick?" Jesse asked.

"I'm not really sure," Rick answered. "We were all sitting around talking and everything was fine. Next thing you know, Howie walked by the window and Susan had a panic attack. She ran into the corner and started to cry and shake uncontrollably. Thank God Neiko was here. He went right over to her and snuggled until she calmed down."

"Oh boy," Jesse said, "she must have seen the person she's afraid of." Jesse walked over to Susan, who was still shaking and sobbing. and sat down on the floor next to her. "Hi Susan, it's okay, don't be scared. Was that man you saw walk by, the one you're afraid of?"

"Yes," Susan sobbed. "That's him. He was there."

"'Where, Susan?" Jesse asked.

"At the accident," she whimpered. "I saw him there."

"Change of plans, people," Jesse said. "Rick, get Tom, the security guard. He's under that brown tarp by the tractor. Tell him to come in here. I have an errand for him."

When Tom arrived, Jesse said, "I need you to go into town for me. There's a one-stop medical center on Route 1 just after the traffic light. Go in there and ask for Dr. Patty Smith. Doctor Smith is a psychologist. Everyone calls her Peppermint Patty. She keeps jars of peppermint candy all around her office. It's like a candy store in there. She specializes in child behavior. The kids love her. Granted she's a real space shot herself—personally, I think all shrinks are. But she's very good at what she does. We've known each other for years and get along great. Tell her I would like her to talk with Susan. I'm sure she can be of some help. If she's not in her office, go to that small pastry place Linda Merten owns on Portland Street. It's called Gretel's Crumb Corner. Linda's always dropping things behind her, like in the story about Hansel and Gretel. That's how the name came about. Ask Linda if Peppermint Patty is there. She likes hanging out with Gretel, to help make the donuts. Hey Tom, while you're there, you might as well bring us back a couple of dozen donuts—they're the best."

Jesse then turned to the others and said, "Okay, folks I guess we know who we were looking for. Shall we wait for him to return?"

* * *

The afternoon passed, with no sign of Howie. Peppermint Patty called Jesse, and said she would be there first thing in the morning.

"I really don't know if he suspects anything's up, but he should be here by now," Jesse said.

"What should we do?" MJ asked.

"I think we just wait it out," Doc responded. "Tom's back undercover outside, and the four of us are inside. Only a fool with a death wish would try anything. I don't believe he's that stupid or brave."

"Okay then let's turn all the lights out, double lock the doors, and wait," Jesse said.

— 6 —

Just a little before daylight, there was a sharp rapping noise on the rec room door. Jesse walked to the door, and looked around to be sure everyone was ready. Rick, MJ, and Doc were spread out facing the door, with their guns in the ready position, just in case. "Remember, Tom is out there," Jesse whispered, "so don't get jumpy." He then grasped the door knob, and with one quick motion pulled it open, switching on the lights as he jumped to the side.

Standing in the doorway, they saw Choo-Choo Charlie holding Howie by the back of his neck.

"Hey guys, look what I found," Charlie snarled. He pushed Howie into the room. His clothes were covered in mud, half his ear was gone, and the side of his face was crusted in blood.

"Holy shit, what happened to him?" Jesse smirked.

"I caught him sneaking into his bunker down back. He didn't expect me to be there, did you, asshole?" Charlie said, as he punched Howie in the ribs, knocking the wind out of him.

"Let me tell you a little story about our friend," Charlie said. "This might take a while. I'll start from the beginning so bear with me. I studied those sketches you had given me, but really couldn't get very much from them except some ideas. I knew the girl was trying to tell us something and I had to put the pieces together. Taking into consideration what little we knew, I took the sketches and went up north to see Squeaky Green. By the way, that girl is really one smart cookie. I studied the accident scene, where her parents had been killed, combined it with the police report and her sketches and started some serious research. This gentlemen is my conclusion . . ."

He cleared his throat and continued, "This is where it gets interesting. Several years ago, the World Trade Towers in New York were attacked by terrorists in a couple of airplanes they had hijacked, remember? Now, it is believed these terrorists came into the United States from Canada. Most likely from a busy crossing area, hoping that confusion would be on their side. We know there are approximately six busy border crossing spots in the town of Houlton, Maine, which is located next to the Canadian border. I-95 and Route 2 are readily available for southbound travel in Houlton, an ideal location. Now what if someone who lived in that area were designated to pick up and transport these terrorists to their next location? This person would also be aware that if any problems were to arise, there was a place for them to go. They would use a bunker that was secretly built, with his supervision, here on this campground. This would be their safety hideout, if needed. It was completely stocked with food, phones, clothes, and a couple of handguns. Now this pickup person would either need some type of van or truck, which he would acquire illegally, to complete his task. Imagine if our driver picked up the terrorist after they successfully crossed the border, and started heading south. Being familiar with the area, and wanting to be as inconspicuous as possible, he decided to take Route 2 through Haynesville. He would then take the Haynesville woods road. He knew that road like the back of his hand. He also knew that with the light coating of snow that had fallen earlier, it could be extremely dangerous. This reassured him that the locals would avoid it if possible, and there should be little traffic. Somewhere along the way, he became tired, and decided to let another driver take over for a short time. We now have a dangerous piece of slippery road, even to those who know it, and an unfamiliar driver. The key ingredients for an accident. And an accident did occur at approximately 7:30 in the evening, that September night, killing Mr. and Mrs. Johnson and leaving their daughter, Susan, injured.

"This would bolster Squeaky Green's theory of the driver being impaired or distracted. In this case distracted due to the fact of not being familiar with the winding slippery road. And the number of occupants would also account for the several sets of footprints found in the snow at the accident scene. Putting all these things together, adding little Susan's sketches and her recognition of someone from the accident, I reached my conclusion. Let me introduce Mohammad Abdul Kazar, also known to you folks as Howard Wang or "Howie" from Houlton, Maine. He's our van driver, extremist, terrorist, and killer. Then Charlie turned and put his knife to Howie's throat and said, "Bye-bye Howie, you asshole."

"No, Charlie!" Doc shouted. "Not this time! We need him to give some testimony at the Pentagon. Let's cuff him up and get him out of here, before I change my mind."

"Today's your lucky day," Charlie snarled at Howie, then in one quick movement, he cut the rest of Howie's ear off and handed it to him.

Doc lunged forward, grabbed the stunned and staggering Howie by the arm, and started for the door. "I have a car coming, Jesse," he said. "I'll be in touch." He stepped outside, got into a black van and was gone.

* * *

"Well guys, that about wraps it up for us, I guess. I'm sure the Feds will be paying a visit soon to close it on their side." Jesse said. "I can't thank you people enough for your help. Rick, make sure you convey that to your maintenance people for me please. Tell everyone to come up here tomorrow for a cookout and campfire on the house. In the meantime, I'll fill Katie and the others in on what happened. Come on MJ, let's go tell them it's over and check on Susan."

* * *

Peppermint Patty arrived at the campground rec room as promised, and Jesse introduced her to Barbie, Ken, and their daughters Lilly and Susan. After a brief discussion, Patty asked if Susan would be comfortable having a talk with her alone. Susan said she would, and they went into the office for some private time. Jesse told the family they were free to leave when they were ready, and urged them to follow any recommendations Patty might have to help Susan resolve the trauma she had experienced.

* * *

That afternoon, after Peppermint Patty and the Johnson family had left the campground, MJ, Katie, and Jesse sat down together in the rec room to chat.

"Who's mixing?"

MJ got up to do the mixing when all of a sudden, he said in a strange tone, "What the— ? I see a deputy out in the field, looking our way."

"Just mix," Katie said to MJ as she took Jesse's hand and said with a smile, "we know he's here."

—7—

Fall and winter came and went, the trees were starting to bud, grass was getting green, and the sound of people and equipment was in the air. "Let's hustle people! One week to opening day and Happy Valley begins another season," Rick shouts.

Katie and Jesse were in the office when they got the news that Susan had spent most of the winter seeing Peppermint Patty, and was doing fine, and the family planned on a visit to the campground in late summer. Doc's arrival was expected any day. They were watching the news on television, when the announcer caught their attention with a special report they found very interesting indeed.

> *The Pentagon has issued a report that a prisoner being transported by government agents has been shot and killed. It appears the prisoner managed to steal a dinner knife from a restaurant as they ate lunch. He then attempted to stab one of the agents, identified only as Mr. Charles. It was further reported that the other agent, identified as Mr. Smith, regrettably had to use deadly force to resolve the situation. The unidentified prisoner later succumbed from gunshot wounds to the body and head.*

—8—

It was a beautiful spring afternoon and the workday was completed. The staff was gathered around the fire pit in the pool area, to have a drink, relax, and discuss the week's work. Katie organized this ritual every Friday afternoon. It gave everyone a little time to iron out problems and vent a little. She tried to stay cognizant of the staff's feelings and problems, knowing they were the backbone of the operation, and that they could make you or break you. That's the main reason the staff was hand-picked.

"Well, boss lady here we go again. Are you ready for it?" Jesse asked Katie with a smile.

"Bring it on," Katie replied. "We're almost booked full for the opening week, first time in years." Usually the first few weeks of the season were slow, with some seasonal residents moving in and getting organized. The transient campers usually started arriving after schools got out for the summer. It's still a busy time—old friends greeting, new friends meeting, along with minor organizing and preparing by the staff. Most of the preparation was finished a few weeks ago but a final tweak is always needed.

About a half hour into the festivities, Bert, the evening and weekend assistant manager, came out of the office and handed Jesse the phone.

"Who is it?" Jesse asked Bert, with a questioning look on his face.

"Squeaky Green," Bert answered, "—said she had a quick question for you."

Jesse took the phone. "Hi Squeak, how's my favorite accident investigator?" The look on his face changed as he got up from his chair and started walking toward the office. "What the hell are you talking about?" I didn't send anyone up there last week." He was still on the phone as he passed Katie and motioned for her to follow him into the office. Jesse finally finished the call and looked at Katie.

"That's not a very happy look on your face," Katie said. "What's up?"

"That was Squeaky Green, she's still up in Haynesville trying to help those folks out with the Johnson accident."

"Okay, I was aware of that," Katie said. "Winter was a bear up there this year and kind of slowed things down. So what's the problem?"

"Squeaky had a meeting yesterday with someone who claimed to have been sent up there by me, to gather new information. She was a little skeptical when he asked her to give him all the information she had collected. He told her he was heading back down and would give it to me. She told him she would have to get it together and he could pick it up tomorrow, then she called me.

"I thought we were through with that," Katie said. "Who did you send up there?"

"I didn't send anyone. I told her to be sure she kept copies of everything and just maybe, leave a few vital things out of what she gave him. When I asked her to describe the person I supposedly sent, guess who she described?"

"Okay, I give up," Katie said. "Tell me."

"How about Howie?" Jesse responded.

Katie took a step back and looked at Jesse like he had two heads as she slipped into a chair. "Howie? Are you serious? I thought he was dead! What's going on for god's sake?"

"Serious as a heart attack," Jesse answered. "We have to get our guys together again and get to the bottom of this. I think the good doctor has the answers we need, and he better be ready to share them. Do me a favor—call MJ and Rick and ask them to meet with us in the morning. I have a really bad feeling about all of this. We may have a bigger problem than we thought."

* * *

Saturday morning, sunny, cool and a beautiful blue sky greeted the day, and Jesse and Katie were at the office bright and early having coffee when Rick arrived.

"Hi, guys, what's up?" He smiled as he poured a cup of coffee.

"We seem to have a few new developments with the Susan scenario that may need some serious looking into. Have you seen MJ yet today?" Jesse asked.

"Actually I have not," Rick replied. "I was down back with that asshole from across the street. We caught him coming through that metal gate in the fence again.

He's always talking to our campers, trying to get them over to his place."

"He's the least of our worries right now," Jesse said. "I just wanted to fill you and MJ in on the latest development about Susan."

"Latest developments?" Rick asked. "I thought that was all over."

"Welcome to the club," Jesse groaned.

The loud ringing of the office phone broke the momentary silence, causing all three of them to jump a little then start laughing. Katie answered it, spoke briefly then hung up with a sigh. "MJ won't be coming, at least for a while. It seems he's working a pretty big case and can't break away, but will give you a call when he can."

"Okay I understand," Jesse said. "Let's fill Rick in on what we know so far, and get his opinion on what's going on." It didn't take Jesse long to brief Rick with the latest information Squeaky Green had given him, leaving Rick sitting in silence, shaking his head.

"Okay let's get the ball rolling," Jesse said. "First things first. Katie, see if you can get the York County Sheriff, Eddie Bell on the phone. Tell whoever answers the phone over there I want to talk to Eddie personally." Jesse and Eddie went back a long way. They had met years ago at the Police Academy Training Center in New Hampshire, where they both instructed firearms training. Eddie was a huge man with hands the size of a catcher's mitt.

"In the meantime Rick and I are going for a little walk down to Howie's alleged bunker and have a look around. You know it just dawned on me that the Feds never did come here for a look around after Doc and Charlie left with the prisoner. I wonder why." Jesse paused. "Let's go have a look Rick."

Jesse and Rick made their way across the field to the drain bunker.

"Hey, do you see what I see? The grass is trampled down as though someone has been here lately," Rick said.

"You're right, Rick! Who the hell knows about this place but us?" They made their way to the entrance door and found it closed just the way they had left it. Jesse nodded to Rick as he took his pistol out of its holster, then with one big push opened the door. Everything looked pretty much the same as it had when they first discovered it. There were a few boxes of dry food and a couple of empty boxes, possibly where the guns and phones had been hidden before Charlie searched the place. "Let's see what we got," Jesse said, opening a few more boxes.

"Well, I'll be damned," Rick said. "Look—It's girls' clothing—what the hell's going on here?"

"Beats the hell out of me," Jesse said. "Keep on looking." They spent an hour opening boxes and looking at contents. They couldn't believe what they saw. The boxes were full of girls' clothing—shoes, sneakers, underwear, jeans, shirts, and sweaters of all sizes. They also found more food, water, and another hand gun that Charlie must have missed.

"Now what?" Rick asked Jesse.

"Just leave things like we found them, except for the gun. Take it. Just a few more questions for the good doctor to answer when he arrives. Let's get out of here and go back to the office."

When they arrived at the office, they were greeted by a giant of a man in a Sheriff's uniform. He grabbed Jesse in a bear hug, lifting him off the floor, and bellowed, "Jesse you old bloodhound, how the hell have you been? As if I didn't already know."

"Holy shit, Eddie! Let me breathe, you beast!" Jesse cried, with a mile-wide grin. Eddie released his grip on Jesse and started laughing.

"And you must be Rick," he said, as they shook hands. "Nice to meet you—heard a lot of good things."

"Nice to meet you, sheriff," Rick replied.

"Call me Eddie—any friend of Jesse and Katie is a friend of mine. Her David worked for me for a while. Hell of a good deputy and hell of a friend. So what can I do for you guys?"

"Well if you remember that problem we had last fall, with the missing girl," Jesse said, "It seems to have resurfaced and doesn't appear to be resolved yet. I have a feeling we're going to have our hands full again, before it's over. And I'm sure you're aware we had a problem with one of your deputies—Billy-Bob—and we really don't want any of that if we can help it."

"I know," Eddie replied. "He can be a real asshole, but I think with a little more experience he will be a good cop. We just need to give him a chance and some guidance."

"I agree Eddie, and I know we overstepped our bounds. Time was a main factor there, and we couldn't screw around with his nonsense. So that brings us to the main reason I called you. Is there any chance you can deputize us so we can have police authority, and cut out the middle man?"

"Well, my friend, that's what I figured this was about. I already ran a background check on you both. I knew there'd be no problem, but it's a necessity and a requirement of the job. So if both of you would raise your right hand and repeat after me, we'll get this show on the road."

After administering the oath of office, Eddie handed Rick and Jesse a badge and identification card. Then with a big smile, said, "Welcome to the York County's Sheriff's Office. Now with that out of the way, how about filling me in on the latest, so I know what to expect."

After Jesse gave Eddie the latest information he had on the case, his heartfelt thanks, and a promise to keep him updated, they all shook hands and Eddie went on his way.

"I guess all we can do now is sit and wait to hear from Squeaky about her meeting this morning with whoever it is that wants the accident information," Jesse said.

"You realize it's after 4:30, so we should be hearing soon," Katie said.

"Where in the hell did the day go?" Rick said with a grin. "Let's have a drink, it's five o'clock somewhere."

Like it was right on cue, the phone rang. "That must be Squeaky calling to fill us in," Jesse said.

Katie and Rick waited intently as Jesse nodded and grunted, while listening to Squeaky fill him in on the latest developments concerning her morning meeting. "Squeaky said there were actually three people talking to her this morning about the accident. One was the person she originally described as Howie, another male she didn't recognize at all, and a woman. She overheard the woman call one of the men Doc. Oh and to top things off, both of the men called her Peachy," Jesse said.

"Oh shit," Katie and Rick said in unison. "Now what's going on?"

"But wait, my fine friends, I saved the best for last. Squeaky heard them talking about two more agents they were expecting. She figures they must be foreign, because one of them is named Neiko. Ring a bell?"

"Oh boy I give up," Rick moaned. "Do we have any more ice? I need another drink."

"Supposedly they should all arrive here in the morning to fill us in on what's going on, Jesse said. "Let's call it a day. We'll meet here at nine o'clock."

Heading back to his camper, Jesse caught the glimpse of a flashlight out in the field. *Well, I'll be darned*, he said to himself. *What do we have here?* Slowly he continued walking, staying in the shadows until he had a good vantage point. He leaned up against the side of an electrical switching station building, where he knew he couldn't be seen, and waited and watched. There it was again, just a quick glimmer of light down by the bunker area, then it was gone. *Gotcha!* he thought—*doing a little shopping?* Jesse thoughtfully made his way back to his camper, trying to make sense out of what he'd seen. He was pretty sure someone was taking things from the bunker, but who and why? *This should be good coffee conservation in the morning*, he thought, as he turned out the light and hoped to get some much needed rest. After a few minutes, he sat up. *I wonder if Rick saw the light too?*

The campground was set up in a large horseshoe type arrangement, with a few short streets inside. Jesse's camper was located at one of the top ends of the shoe, while Rick's was located at the other top end. Tom, the security guard, was camped at the lower center of the shoe. This arrangement gave each of them the ability to view the campground from three different angles. In the event there was an emergency or a problem, one of them could detect it and respond easily. Although problems were almost unheard of at Happy Valley, it was good to be prepared, just in case.

—9—

Morning finally arrived and as usual was bright, sunny and cool. The staff was hustling around laughing and joking as they prepared for another day. Jesse was heading to the office door just as Rick and Tom rounded the corner.

"Morning guys," Jesse said. "You didn't happen to see anything unusual last night, did you?"

"As a matter of fact we both did," Rick replied.

"Actually it happened twice," Tom said, "and I wrote down the times just in case it would help."

"Perfect," Jesse said. "Let's go in, get a coffee and compare notes."

The trio were pouring their coffee when Katie came through the door. "Hi guys, we have company," she said. Following right behind her were Doc, Peachy, Howie, MJ, and Neiko.

"Well, well, look what the cat dragged in," Jesse moaned. "I think somebody owes us an explanation. Of course not you, Howie. You're dead, right?"

"Okay," Doc replied, "let me explain."

"Explain my ass!" Jesse yelled. "No more damn lies Doc. We trusted you and you left us hanging out to dry. What about you, MJ—were you in on this?"

"I had no idea. I was sent up to Haynesville yesterday by Homeland Security, and instructed to meet with Doc and his crew," MJ said.

"Hold it people, let's all sit down and calm down," Rick

said. "This isn't getting us anywhere. Okay, Doc let's hear it, and it better be good."

"When this thing all started, I put some feelers out to try and get a handle on the situation. Believe it or not, we all don't share information like one would expect. It's kind of like spoiled kids with a new toy. Finally after our collective investigation here, and a little help from Choo-Choo Charlie, we got a break. Once we knew Susan was alive and well, we understood the situation here had to be closed quickly, so as not to arouse suspicion regarding what we thought we had discovered. I sincerely apologize to you, my friends for deceiving you, but it was a necessity as you will see. After Charlie met with Squeaky Green, we were pretty sure of what we had, and needed a plan. Then after searching the bunker and discovering the clothes, we were positive. Charlie deliberately didn't let on that he found the clothing when he went into his rant about Howie. We intended on filling you in, but then Susan recognized Howie that day and we had to move fast. We wanted all eyes and connection with this place to come to an end. Now just so you know, Howie was certainly at the accident that killed Susan's mom and dad, but it was after it took place, and Susan definitely recognized him. If you remember she was near death, when an alert EMT was able to see signs of life, and ended up saving her. The EMT, my friends, was none other than Howie—that's when she saw him. Howie's real name is Richie Patterson. He's been living undercover for the agency as Howard Wang, a low-life loner, in Houlton, Maine, for the past several years. It was his knowledge of the area and a great imagination that helped us come up with our terrorist story in record time."

Doc paused to let all this sink in, before continuing. "Now we are still not sure whether the accident could have been prevented, and are still working on that. The van was in fact carrying women against their will to an undisclosed location. We have reason to believe that the Johnsons—Susan's parents—had stumbled upon this human trafficking ring and intended to report it to the sheriff. Instead they ended up as collateral damage, if you know what I mean? And by the way, that whole Howie scene Charlie put on at the end was fake. Fake blood, fake ear, fake everything. Actually, he says he deserves an academy award for it. Oh, and I wrote the fake news announcement."

Doc took a moment to clear his throat, and said, "Yesterday, Agent Keene and myself joined Charlie and Howie, and all met with Squeaky in Haynesville. When we were sure of what we had, we contacted Homeland Security and requested MJ and Neiko join us. We wanted to be sure we didn't miss anything. When MJ finished there he had to go back and brief the governor. This is a major breakthrough. That brings us up to date. The next big question is: Where are the women? We believe the clothes and food in the bunker is intended for them. Obviously they're being held somewhere nearby, waiting for the camp to reopen for the season. That's about it gentlemen, I will be glad to answer any questions you have. We have no more secrets. I truly apologize for the deception and hope you understand the reasoning behind it. I also hope that we can remain friends," Doc finished quietly.

"I have a question," Jesse said. "What about the bunker? How come Howie helped build it in the first place?"

"That was a key development in the case," Doc said. "This trafficking ring has been operating for a long time, and after a couple of long years of trying, Howie was able to get a foot in the door. Things were going fine for a while until one of the rings' travel routes started to get questionable, and was closed down. Knowing they had to find a new route, Howie stepped up with a plan, they bought it, and the bunker idea became a reality. He would lure them here and hopefully shut them down, at least for a while."

"You knew about the bunker all along?" Jesse asked.

"Not at all—it was a surprise to me. I didn't even know

about Howie until Charlie uncovered him," Doc answered. "I always considered him a scumbag. I guess his cover worked—at least on me."

"Well, Doc, I think I'm speaking for all of us when I say we're not in a popularity contest. We do what we have to do, at the time a problem arises. If everything were perfect, the world wouldn't need guys like us to be watch dogs. That being said, let's grab lunch and share a little new information that has just developed," Jesse said.

They headed out to Gretel's, ordered their food, and settled in to hear what Jesse had to say.

"Well, we had the lights appear in the field again last night," Jesse said. "Rick and I saw them once. Tom saw them twice and noted the times. It was the same scenario as before, on for a short period and then disappear."

"Perfect. Maybe they're getting ready to make their move and are checking the place out. Don't forget, they are well aware of the episode with Charlie and Howie, and are under the assumption that Howie is dead. That means they're going to be a little cautious at first, but once they think it's safe they will make their move. Let's make a plan. We don't want to get anxious and blow this chance to get them," Doc cautioned.

"I'm open for all suggestions, let's talk it out guys, this shit has to stop," Jesse said.

"Okay," Doc said. "How about we have a couple of guys hiding by the entrance, and one in the lower field. Then we have someone down by the sliding gate, with a radio, to give us a heads up when they enter?"

"Sounds pretty good to me," Jesse replied. "We don't have a lot of choices, you know."

"Anyone else have thoughts on this?" Doc asked.

"Should we call the sheriff and advise him?" Rick asked.

"It wouldn't hurt to keep him informed," Jesse answered.

"Remember, we don't know if this is the real deal or just wishful thinking on our part."

"How about we do a dry run and just observe what's going on?" Tom asked. "It should also help us decide how we're going to handle the real thing, when and if it happens."

"Yes," Doc responded. "Great idea. Let's see what we really are dealing with. It could just be kids from next door screwing off."

"Okay then, if no one else has anything, let's get organized and give it a go," Jesse said.

"Remember, dry run or not, this could be dangerous, so be prepared for anything."

"Let's decide who goes where and when, then get this thing going. Your place, your call," Doc said to Jesse.

"Okay, Doc, I'd like you and Peachy right up by the bunker. You can position yourselves at a good vantage point where you feel comfortable. Rick, you and I in the middle area spread out a little, but in sight of each other. Tom, I want you down by the fence gate. It might be a little tricky to find a good spot, maybe in a tree if necessary. Take some camo, a light, radio, handgun, and vest from the security office downstairs. You can head down there anytime you're ready. Be careful, take no chances. The rest of us should grab some gear and get ready."

"Okay," Tom replied. Let's get into position about an hour before dark so we can see what we're doing. What about radio checks?"

"Good thinking, Tom, how about 8:30, then none until necessary," Jesse answered.

"Copy that," Tom answered and headed to the security office to grab his gear.

* * *

The clouds had overtaken the moon, and it was so dark you could hardly see your hand in front of you. Everyone was in position, waiting and listening silently. At exactly 8:30, the silence was suddenly broken, when their radios crackled.

"Radio check, if you copy just double click when I say your name," Tom whispered. Tom recited all the team members names and got the response he had requested. This assured him everyone was on the right channel and ready to receive messages. Now it was nothing but a waiting game.

A little after 10:30 the radios came to life again. "Heads up," Tom whispered. "I have movement at the gate. I have a visual of six figures making their way into the field. It appears to be two males, and four females connected together with a rope of some sort, heading your way." Jesse and Rick waited until the six passed their positions, then they slipped in behind them and began to follow. Just then the radio came to life again. "Wait—here comes two more males, I can hear them talking. I'm pretty sure one of them just said they had to finish tonight," Tom whispered.

The second message came too late for Jesse and Rick to stop, they had already turned their radios down, fallen in line behind the suspects, and were almost at the bunker. Time seemed to stand still. Everyone froze. Then a few sharp words from one of the men and the bunker door opened. There was a flicker of light, and the women were forced inside.

Jesse and Rick had followed the group as far as they could, trying to keep a safe distance, then stopped and crouched down. They watched in silence as the bunker opened and closed, contemplating what would happen next. Their thoughts were answered almost immediately. Jesse heard a sound behind him and as he started to turn, he felt the cold steel barrel of a gun being pressed up against the back of his neck.

"Move and you're dead," a voice said. Jesse remained completely still, as he was instructed. He realized the two subjects Tom had warned them about, had caught up with them. Off to his right he saw movement, heard another noise, then saw Rick being led his way, also at gunpoint. "Move," the voice said again, and pushed Jesse and Rick inside the bunker.

The bunker was lit up by large Coleman lanterns, leaving a sort of ghostly glow. The four women, whose ages appeared to be between sixteen and twenty, were seated on a bench. They were tied together chain gang style, with a large rope looped around their waists. The fear in their eyes said it all, as they huddled together.

Jesse recognized the two men that had captured himself and Rick. It was none other than Stanley and Harvey Fielding, the owners of the campground next door. Things were finally starting to make sense to Jesse. He just hoped it wasn't too late.

"Well, McGraw, you and Twinkle Toes here," he said, pointing at Rick, "had to keep sticking your noses into things. Now look what it's going to get you," Stanley snarled.

"Okay you guys, get the girls outfitted and back to the camp. Whatever clothes are left. put them in the van," Harvey said to the other two men. When the women finished changing their clothes, they were tied back together, and led out the door.

"Okay, Batman and Robin, I'm gonna love this," Stanley said, as he pushed Jesse and Rick out the door and onto the ground.

No sooner had they hit the ground, when two shots rang out, followed by a brief silence. "Hey, Batman and Robin, you okay?" Doc called out.

"What the hell happened?" Jesse asked.

"I don't know for sure. Me and Peachy saw the door fly open, and you two fell out. Next thing we saw these two guys pointing guns at you and laughing, so we had no choice but to take them out," Doc said.

"Look down there, blue lights," Peachy said, as she pointed down toward the fence gate.

"Hey, Jesse," a voice rang out. "It's me, Eddie Bell, are you guys okay?"

"Yes, we're fine Eddie," Jesse responded. "How did you know we needed you?"

"Your security guard Tom gave us a call after he saw a couple of subjects you didn't expect headed your way, and thought a little back-up might be in order. We have the other ones all rounded up down below and are waiting for a warrant to go visit next door to see what's left," Eddie said.

"The owner and his brother are up here, Eddie, but the only one they will be seeing is the medical examiner. You might want to make the call," Jesse said.

"Okay, we got it from here. Stop by for statements later," Eddie answered.

"Okay, Eddie, will do, thanks again." Jesse then turned to the other three and said, "Let's go, gang, I think we all need a drink . . . You too, ghost!"

The four of them turned and started for the main area of the camp when a familiar voice filled the air. "If you guys are thinking of going for a drink, forget about it. You're not going anywhere, besides dead men don't drink," said the voice.

"What the hell, Howie is that you?" Doc asked.

"Sorry, Doc, six long years of living, working, and acting like a low life has put me in a very profitable position, and I kinda like it. I make as much in one delivery of these girls as you make in a year. It just wouldn't be reasonable to let you end it now. Those Fielding brothers and their so-called campground were nothing but a place for me to hide the girls for a short time. Sort of like a stagecoach stop, if you know what I mean. Besides, you saved me having to end it for them. Today was going to be their last day, and ammo is expensive, you know. Oh and Doc, one more thing, that cute girl with the limp has an appointment with Peppermint Patty tomorrow. She doesn't know it yet but that's the last one. I'm taking her with me. I know a big fat sheik that will pay big bucks for her, limp and all. I'm so glad I saved her life," Howie smirked.

Suddenly, Jesse became enraged, lunged at Howie, lost his footing, stumbled and fell to the ground. Howie turned to fire his weapon at Jesse, saw Doc drawing his weapon, and fired a shot hitting Doc in the forearm. Simultaneously two shots rang out, both hitting Howie sending him sprawling, dead on the ground.

"You guys alright?" MJ yelled as he and Choo Choo Charlie came running down the embankment. "We got here as fast as we could. Lucky we saw that deputy on the hill waving his arms at us or we would have gone the wrong way."

"There's no deputies here. They all left with Eddie Bell," Rick said, as he shook his head and looked at the others with a grin.

"We thought you and Charlie had gone back to file reports," Jesse said.

"We did, but when we started talking with other team members and after comparing information, we realized what was really going on with Howie. It seems new things that couldn't be explained kept turning up and pointing a finger in his direction. By the end of the meeting we realized he had to be our man. So we packed up and headed here to warn you before something happened," MJ explained.

"Lucky for us, you guys saved our bacon and maybe the lives of a lot of young women. At least a few we know of." Jesse replied.

"I see blue lights coming. Let's get Doc patched up, head back to the office and get this stuff on paper. I'll call Eddie Bell and fill him in. Let's go. You coming, ghost?" Jesse said with a smile.

~ Part 2 ~

—10—

It was the end of another wonderful season at Happy Valley. The itinerant campers had all gone home, and the more permanent campers were packed and ready to head out.

It had been a very interesting season. The most unprecedented incident in the history of the campground had been resolved, and the camp was officially closing for the year.

Rick, the lead maintenance man, and his crew, had secured all the outdoor furniture and equipment. Water and electricity were shut down and the gates closed and locked. The skeleton crew that stayed behind to accomplish this task had just finished packing their bags and vehicles, and were saying their farewells, until next spring. MJ was on his way to New Hampshire for a meeting with the governor. Rick was pulling out with his motorhome, heading to sunny Arizona for the winter. Katie, who lives here in southern Maine, was finishing up her paperwork, getting ready to take a few weeks' vacation in Florida, then return to the campground in to start all over again. Doc and Peachy had already left, gone who knows where.

Meanwhile, Jesse had no intention of going anywhere further than his cabin in New Hampshire. He was a firm believer that one of the best things about living in New England is the changing of the seasons. Mother Nature has a way of amazing you, pleasing you, and frustrating you—quite often all in the same day. True New Englanders accept this as a way of life—not letting it phase them in the least, knowing that if they wait a while, things are always changing.

These wistful thoughts were in Jesse McGrath's mind as he sat on the porch of his secluded log cabin, watching the multi-colored fall leaves dance in the golden sunlight, under a dazzlingly blue, picture-perfect late fall sky. *It can't get any better than this,* he said to himself, as he cracked open an ice cold beer and smiled. Jesse's cabin sat in the middle of a forty acre lot in northern New Hampshire, surrounded by the White Mountain National Forest.

Jesse inherited the cabin from a friend he and one of his best friends, Rick Smith, had served with, while they were acting as military advisors in Vietnam. His name was Dan O'Riley, and like Jesse and Rick, he was also an Airborne Ranger. His friends fondly referred to him as "Danny the Lion," because of his fearlessness. Dan was caught in an enemy trap early one dreary rain-soaked morning, while he was attempting to rescue some small children that appeared to be pinned down by enemy fire. Unfortunately, his efforts were in vain and he was wounded several times. Jesse had rushed to Dan's aid under heavy enemy fire, but to no avail. He was wounded twice trying to pull Dan out of the line of fire. Both Jesse and Dan were ultimately dragged to safety by Rick, but it was too late to save Dan.

After Jesse's return from Vietnam, Dan's family insisted Jesse take the cabin. They said Dan would have wanted it that way.

The cabin was a perfect refuge. Electricity was piped underground from somewhere near the interstate. It boasted a drilled well, oversized septic system and a whole house generator for emergencies. This was where Jesse spent most of his time, when he wasn't on duty as chief of security at Happy Valley. The season's end did not hurt Jesse's feelings one bit—he was more than ready for a rest. He enjoyed being alone and spending his time sitting on his cabin porch, watching the weather change, drinking a few beers and now and then using the empty beer cans for entertaining target practice.

Occasionally his campground co-worker and close friend

Rick Smith, along with Doc and Peachy, visit and spend a few days.

Jesse's thoughts were interrupted by the ringing of the phone. He immediately made a mental note to shoot the damn phone the next chance he got. He considered it a nuisance.

"It better be good," he answered. "I'm not interested in buying, selling, contributing, or sponsoring anything, so who is this and what do you want?"

"Don't be a crab, Jesse," a familiar voice responded. "It's me, Katie, I had a strange incident here at the campground that I wanted to discuss with you, so lose the attitude for a minute," she chuckled.

"Hi, Katie, hearing your voice, just made a near perfect day . . . perfect. Now tell me what earth-shattering incident can happen at an empty campground? Broken water pipe?" Jesse responded with a chuckle, as he popped open another ice cold beer.

As Katie began to relate what had happened, the phone beeped in Jesse's ear. Someone else was calling. Jesse looked at the incoming number and said, "Hang on a minute, Katie. Doc is trying to get me on the other line." And he put Katie on hold.

"Hello my friend, what's the good word?" Jesse asked. "The gun that was stuck in my face didn't go off," Doc replied. "Thanks to Peachy's quick thinking."

"Holy shit! If that's the good news, I have got to hear the bad. Hang on, I have Katie on the other line, and I'll have her call back."

"No, finish your conversation with Katie. I don't think my problem is going anywhere for a while. Call back later when we can talk," Doc replied, and hung up.

"Hi Katie, I'm back. Sorry about the interruption. It seems Doc has a real problem down there in Snow-Bird-land and may need a little help."

"No problem," Katie replied. "Actually the incident here may have a little bearing on whatever is going on with Doc."

"You certainly have my full attention now, Katie. What the hell's going on up there in Happy Valley that could affect Doc in Snow-Bird-land?"

"You might as well get yourself another cold one. This is going to take a while. Ttell me when you're ready."

"Okay smarty, I'm all set let me hear it."

Katie began describing what had recently happened early one evening at the campground entrance. It all began when Billy Murphy, her chief of maintenance, was on his way to an emergency plumbing call on the same street as the campground. As Billy passed the campground entrance, he noticed a blue SUV parked in a secluded corner near the main building. Not really sure who owned the vehicle, or why it was there, he decided to call Katie on his cell phone just to let her know about it.

Under normal circumstances, Billy would have stopped. He was the go-to guy at the campground. If he had not been about to attend to a major water leak at the nearby nursing home, he would have stopped to checked the vehicle. He knew teenagers would, on occasion, park there, drink beer, or make out, so he wasn't that concerned. He also knew Katie would have no problem sending them on their way. Everyone in the area knew Billy, and if he told you to move on, it would be in your best interest to do so. Jesse had called on Billy a few months ago to help locate some teenage troublemakers from a nearby campground that he suspected of causing a problem. Considering that Billy had dragged one of them by the ear, partially tearing it off, the incident was taken care of without much trouble.

Katie continued filling Jesse in on the parked car incident. She told him how, as she approached the campground, the vehicle Billy had told her about, was just leaving. Wondering what was going on, she ran after the vehicle and pounded on the window.

The driver, a woman with long blonde hair, shouted, "Sorry! I won't park there anymore," and sped off. Satisfied the problem was solved, Katie said she then did a quick walk around the office building, saw nothing out of the ordinary, and went home.

"Okay, sounds like you solved the problem—if that's all that happened. What makes you think it might have some bearing on Doc?" Jesse asked.

"Well, the next day when I went to the office to check the mail and telephone messages, just my usual daily routine, I noticed one of the windows didn't look completely closed. I checked the security cameras and sure enough, someone had been inside. I also found the file cabinet that contained personal information on the permanent residents was half-open, and the file with Doc and Peachy's home address was lying on top."

"Oh boy, things are beginning to get interesting," Jesse replied. "I have a bad feeling this may have something to do with the incident Doc just had, let's hope not."

"Are you thinking the same as I am? That someone is trying to locate Doc, and broke into my files to get his winter address?" Katie asked.

"Maybe that's just what they were after," Jesse said. "When Doc called earlier, he didn't really give me any details of what was going on, but he told me enough to pique my interest. I'll be giving him a call back shortly."

"Okay Jesse, will you be coming here, and is there anything I should do?" Katie asked.

"Yes, I'll be up after I get in touch with Doc and find out exactly what happened down there. Did you call Eddie Bell and fill him in on the break-in?" Jesse asked.

"Yes I did, as soon as I realized someone had been in here. Eddie sent a crew over and they took pictures, dusted for prints, and reviewed the security cameras. Unfortunately there were no prints found. Oh, and Jesse—I forgot to mention—I also took a picture of the vehicle's license plate as it was leaving that night. I shared it with Eddie."

"Perfect, Katie, I was pretty sure you would have done that," Jesse responded. He knew that the wives of policemen, deputies, and most law enforcement officers all seemed to have the same instincts as their husbands. When a possible incident would arise, their reaction would usually be the right one, as it was in this instance—to make note of any details—like taking a picture of the license plate.

"With any luck, we'll find the owner of the plate. I'll give you a call or be up there shortly. First, I have to talk to Doc and find out exactly what's going on down there."

Jesse looked at the clock he kept mounted on the mantel. The clock was shaped like a police badge—black with a thin blue line. The Thin Blue Line, distinguishing law and order from chaos. It was a constant reminder of how precious but fragile law, order, and life could be. Where the hell did the time go—a little after midnight, but not too late to call Doc. That man never seems to sleep.

Jesse dialed the good doctor up, and it was no surprise it was answered on the first ring. Some things never change.

"Well hello there," the very pleasant voice of Peachy purred. "We were expecting your call. How have you been?" Peachy was Doc's friendly, good-looking, girlfriend. Only a chosen few knew she also worked for the agency, although she would deny any affiliation. Quick-tempered, extremely smart, and almost fearless, her friendly appearance revealed none of those hidden qualities. "Doc will be right with you," she said, before Jesse could answer her. "He's mixing us drinks at the present time."

Jesse smiled to himself and said, "No worries, Peachy, I'd rather talk to you anyway, and you must know by now, that I would never interrupt a man making a drink."

Seconds later, the familiar low-key, matter-of-fact voice of

Doc came on the line. "Hello my friend, glad you called back. It seems someone down here doesn't like me."

Jesse marveled at Doc's unruffled attitude. In all the years they had known each other, he had never seen Doc let anything bother or upset him—not even having a gun stuck in his face. Jesse remembered how the two of them, along with Peachy and Rick, were being held at gunpoint not so long ago. Before it was over, Doc ended up being wounded, but it didn't seem to faze him. He just took it in stride, and acted as though it happened every day.

"Hello my friend, what the hell is going on down there in Snow-Bird-land?" I can't leave you alone for five minutes without you getting involved in some kind of trouble. You're starting to act like MJ," Jesse said jokingly.

"Well, the other night Peachy and I were returning home from dinner and it appears someone tried to set me up by staging a fake accident. We were heading down the coast road, just beyond the beach where there are several pull-offs for ocean watchers. We rounded a bend in the road and came up behind a car halfway off the travel portion of the road, with a couple of girls in it. We stopped and asked if they were alright and they said yes, they were fine, but maybe I should check the truck of the car in front of them, which was well off the road—lights on and motor running. Peachy and I ran up to the truck, and when I looked in the open window, I saw that the man in the driver's seat was slumped down. I leaned into the truck to speak with him and all at once, Peachy yelled, "Gun!" and grabbed the man's arm, just as he stuck the gun in my face. If Peachy hadn't been there and reacted, I probably wouldn't be talking to you now. Fortunately, another car had stopped to see if they could be of any assistance, and when they saw what was happening, they called the police, and helped me subdue the gunman until the police arrived. What's really odd, is when I glanced back toward the first vehicle—the one the girls were in—it was gone. They had taken off."

"That definitely seems odd, Doc. They may have been involved in some way, and when they saw things going wrong, they knew enough to take off," Jesse answered.

"That's exactly what I was thinking. But it beats the hell out of me what the whole thing is about. As you're well aware of, we only got here about three weeks ago, and haven't seen or talked to anyone except family and close friends."

Doc and Peachy spent their winters in a beautifully landscaped and well-maintained condominium complex in Fort Myers, Florida. The complex was just far enough away from the hustle and bustle of the sun worshippers, yet conveniently located near shopping, beach going, and an occasional night on the town. Their summers were spent at Happy Valley campground, where they owned a modest park model camper.

"I have a bad feeling this incident may be a little more involved than you know. Let me tell you why." Jesse told Doc about the break-in at Happy Valley campground, and how it involved a blue SUV and the young blonde driver—and how Katie had found Doc's address file outside of its file folder when she went to the office the next day. "I have a suspicion this is more than a coincidence, Doc. I'm heading to Maine in the morning to see what I can find out. I hope my gut feeling is wrong, but I suspect you may very well be the hunted, not the hunter. I'll be in touch, as soon as I do a little more checking on things up there. In the meantime you and Peachy better watch your backs. I'll put in a call to MJ and Rick and fill them in on what's been going on, so hang tight," Jesse said, and hung up the phone.

Jesse put in a quick call to MJ and Rick, but his calls went right to voicemail, so he left a message for them to call him when they were available. He wanted to brief them on the problems at Happy Valley and Doc's incident. He also knew MJ was busy as hell with the Internet Crimes Against Children program, and that Rick was somewhere in Arizona on vacation. Busy or vacationing, Jesse wanted to contact them and make them aware of what was going on.

Although Rick and MJ were not obligated in any way to get involved, there was a special brotherhood bond between Jesse, Rick, and MJ, formulated by the many years of working and investigating numerous cases together. Without question, this made them a formidable team whenever they joined forces.

Another one of Jesse's quirks, you might say, was his firm belief, and he often made it very clear—acquaintances and friends are different from each other. The difference is most evident, he would say, when a person gets in a serious or emergency situation, and has to call for some sort of assistance. It's your friends that will drop everything to help—you can count them. Your acquaintances are usually too busy or don't want to get involved. With all that being said, anything involving Katie or Doc, who were both counted as among his closest friends, was considered of ultimate concern to all of them, and they would react without hesitation.

Jesse cracked another cold beer, got a bag of chips out of the pantry, settled into his favorite chair and planned his trip back to Maine. Not being in a big hurry and needing to think things out, he decided he would take the scenic route. He disliked the Interstates anyway. He would take Route 3 into Whitefield and stop at one of his favorite haunts, Gramma's Kitchen, a small old fashioned restaurant nestled between Lancaster and Twin Mountain. The place wasn't fancy, but the food was good and the waitstaff made you feel like they really enjoyed you being there—sort of a warm feeling of being home. He would have some breakfast, then continue through Lancaster, Groveton, and Colebrook, then up Route 26 to L.L. Cote in Errol. He could pick up some supplies at L.L. Cote—they sold everything imaginable there. This would also give him a chance to visit with the Cotes, as they had been friends for years. After his visit he would head for Maine via Route 16. He knew he could pick up Route 153 in Conway and follow it to Route 109, which would take him into Maine.

Jesse liked taking his time when he was figuring things out. He could let his mind wander and play the question and answer game with himself, concerning whatever case or incident he may be involved with. He felt this helped him make reasonable decisions, separating what he knew for sure, from what he assumed and needed to verify. Obviously, he didn't have much to go on concerning whether Doc's or Katie's incidents were connected. That remained to be seen. They could have absolutely nothing to do with each other, while on the other hand, they could be totally related. Taking into consideration the type of work Doc was involved in, and the fact his file appeared to be the only one that had been disturbed at Happy Valley, anything was possible. There was no question all aspects needed to be looked into, and that's just what Jesse intended to do.

Jesse leaned his head back, and closed his eyes. He loved this old chair, it was like a true old friend, it helped him think clearly. As relaxation set in and sleep began to take over, the silence was broken by ringing. "Damn phone," Jesse sputtered, as he threw the phone across the room. It just missed the fireplace and landed softly on bags he had packed for his trip. Jesse dragged himself out of his chair and slowly retrieved the phone. "Who the hell is this, and what do you want?" he answered.

"Hey! I wish you'd stop throwing the phone when I'm on it," the familiar sound of MJ's voice on the other end replied.

"What makes you think I threw the phone?" Jesse grumbled.

"Because you were probably sipping a beer, or half asleep in your chair. It's 3:30 in the morning and you hate the phone to begin with. Tell me I'm wrong," MJ laughed. "I just got your message. What in the hell is going on—do you need me to come up?"

"Actually, I just wanted you and Rick to be aware of a couple of strange incidents that have taken place—one involving Katie and one involving Doc. Really not sure yet if there's any connection between the two, but I have a gut feeling there may be. I know how busy you are, but if you have any free time it would be great to have you around. I'm heading for Maine when daylight rolls around."

"Well it just so happens I do have some free time. The governor has closed everything down for a couple of weeks, hoping it will help with the damn Covid problem. Where do you want to meet? I assume you're not taking the highway."

"Right you are, I'm taking the scenic route, stopping at Gramma's Kitchen to eat, then up to L.L. Cote, get some supplies, visit, then jump on Route 16." Jesse answered.

"Okay, I'll meet you for breakfast at Gramma's, the best damn food around, you know. I can follow you to Cote's, leave my truck there and jump in with you. That way we can toss this thing around. I kind of figured you might like some help. I'm all packed and I will be out the door in about five minutes," MJ said.

"Great! I was hoping you might be able to break away for a while. I have a feeling this could be a tough one to figure out. I'll see you at Gramma's, besides it's your turn to buy," Jesse snickered as he hung up, settled into his chair, and closed his eyes.

A little after six the next morning Jesse locked up the camp, threw his bag into his truck, and headed north to meet MJ at Gramma's Kitchen for breakfast. As he pulled into the parking lot, he was surprised but pleased to find MJ already there waiting for him. They went inside, found a corner table and placed their order. Jesse wasted no time filing MJ in on what little information he had concerning what was going with Katie and Doc. MJ sat and looked out the window for a few minutes then turned and said, "The plate Katie took a picture of, where was it from, do we know?"

"Actually I don't. She told me she shared it with Eddie Bell, but I haven't had a chance to talk to him yet. Let me give him a call right now," Jesse answered. Jesse went outside for privacy, called the York, Maine, sheriff's office, and spoke with his old friend, Sheriff Eddie Bell. He asked Eddie if he had any information he could share, regarding the aforementioned license plate. When he returned inside he just sat and looked out the window for a few minutes with a puzzled look on his face. Then he wrote something on a napkin and pushed it over to MJ.

"Holy shit, are you kidding me? Is this some kind of a joke or something? I don't believe it," MJ said, with a shocked look on his face.

Jesse just shrugged his shoulders as he finished the last of his coffee, staring out the window. "If you're ready, we might as well get going. We should be at Cote's in a little more than an hour," and he headed for the door. MJ paid the waitress and followed Jesse. Both men got in their respective vehicles, nodded to each other, and headed north. This was destined to be an interesting trip, to say the least. Both men would be racking their respective brains, trying to make sense of the license plate information they had received from Eddie Bell.

Just about two hours from the time they left Gramma's Kitchen, Jesse and MJ arrived at Cote's in Errol. The ride was uneventful and relatively smooth, with a few minor stops for construction and a moose or two crossing the road as the only highlights of the trip. After lunch with their friends and some shopping for supplies, they loaded all MJ's gear into Jesse's truck, pulled it to the back of the parking lot, got out, sat on the tailgate, and cracked an ice cold beer from MJ's cooler. "It's time to relax and think my friend," MJ quipped, as he smiled and raised his bottle in a toast to Jesse. The two finished their beer in silence, closed the tailgate, climbed up into the cab and headed to Maine.

The two sat quietly staring out the window, watching

nothing in particular, but seeing everything and making mental notes as they rode along. This type of behavior isn't unusual for police officers—it's a matter of habit. They ride or have ridden in patrol cars for hours, either alone or with a partner, watching, listening, thinking, trying not to make hasty decisions or draw conclusions to any problems that arise. And also trying to remember to pick up their dry cleaning or bring home a loaf of bread, and numerous other things, later. Alone or with a partner, they are alone until they are called upon to react, then they are a team. MJ and Jesse are a prime example of this. They don't need to speak to know what the other one's thinking.

Shortly after crossing the state line into Maine, MJ asked Jesse to pull over at a small plaza they were approaching, so he could get out and stretch his legs and pick up a snack. Jesse pulled the truck into the rather crowded parking lot, found a spot in a far corner, and parked. MJ went into the store and returned with some snacks and a cold beer for each of them.

Jesse looked at MJ for a minute and then said, "Okay, I give up . . . What?"

"You didn't happen to notice that blue Blazer as we pulled around back, did you?" MJ asked.

"You mean the one with the blacked out windows and the scrape on the driver's door—the same one that was at Gramma's Kitchen and Cote's?"

"Yup that's the one, my observant friend. I figured you did. I first saw it at Grammas. It seemed to appear out of nowhere and was paying particular attention to your truck. Then I saw it again at Cote's. That's why I popped the tailgate and got us a beer. I wanted to watch for a while, but it disappeared again. Interesting isn't it. Should we see what they want?" MJ said with a smile.

"No, let's let them think we haven't seen them. I'm curious about what they're up to also, and why they're interested in us. There's a long stretch of isolated road up ahead. I'll slow down a little and see if they want to make some kind of a move. You do have your gun on you, right?" Jesse asked, already knowing the answer. In their line of work, guns were like underwear—you'd feel half-dressed without them. MJ just sat there looking out the window smiling and thinking to himself, *that's a stupid question. I won't even respond and he knows it.*

Jesse kept the truck speed to between 45 and 50, anticipating the blue Blazer that had been following them to make a move, but it was no longer in sight. "Looks like our friends have lost interest in us, at least for now. Must be playing a little cat and mouse," he said to MJ.

They continued traveling north, occasionally bouncing a question off each other, otherwise just looking straight ahead and thinking. All at once the silence was interrupted by the ringing of MJ's phone. He grabbed it off the dashboard before Jesse could throw it out the window, and answered it. After a brief conversation and a few grunts and okay's, he hung up, turned to Jesse, and smiled. "That was Squeaky Green for you. It seems your phone isn't working or it may be turned off. She said she tried to call you a couple of times."

Squeaky's actual name was Marie, but the nickname Squeaky was given to her by fellow investigators she has worked with over the years. Along with being a friend, Squeaky was a top-notch accident investigator and reconstructionist who had done work for Jesse on many occasions.

"She said Rick called her last night after he couldn't get in touch with you. He wanted to let you know he was on his way. He was taking the red-eye from Phoenix to Portland and wanted us to pick him up on the way to camp. Oh, and he also told her to remind you to turn on your damn phone. Actually I spoke with Squeaky last night, just before I called you, and she told me she was heading north today and agreed to take Neiko to a groomer appointment for me this morning, then drop him off with Katie on her way up. That made it possible for me to meet you earlier, and not have to wait for him. He should have already been dropped off with Katie by the time we get there," MJ said.

* * *

Later that afternoon, just as the sun was beginning to flicker behind the trees, Jesse eased his big F-350 Ford pickup truck into the parking lot adjacent to the Portland, Maine, International JetPort Air Terminal. Jesse estimated their travel time to the campground from there was only about thirty minutes, so there was no need to hurry. They would arrive long before dark, although it really didn't matter. First things first, they had to find Rick.

Just then a voice bellowed, "Hey Jesse and MJ, over here in the lounge." It was Rick standing on a stool wearing a cowboy hat, tank top shirt, cowboy boots, and shorts.

"Must have been hot in Arizona," MJ quipped to Jesse as they made their way to Rick.

After a few handshakes and high fives the trio found a table in the corner of the room, ordered a cold pitcher of beer and some chicken wings. After they finished eating, Jesse told Rick he really hadn't expected him to come all the way from Arizona—he just wanted him to be aware that something was going on.

"You had no choice, my friend. I'm supposed to be here," Rick smiled. So bring me up to date on what was going on with Doc and Katie." Jesse gave Rick a quick rundown of what they knew, which was very little. Then he showed Rick the napkin he'd written on, with the owner of the license plate Katie had taken a picture of. Rick's mouth fell open and he just stared at Jesse in disbelief.

"Oh, there's one other thing," Jesse continued. He then mentioned the blue Blazer that appeared to be following him and MJ. "Maybe absolutely nothing and has no connection at all but it certainly is strange to say the least. Anyway we should get going, just talking about it isn't going to get it figured out. I hope you have more clothes with you than you have on, Tex!" Jesse laughed, and they started out of the terminal toward the truck.

"Hey Jesse, don't look now, but it looks like our friends are back. I believe that's our blue Blazer parked over by the baggage terminal door," MJ said in a low voice. Jesse casually glanced in that direction and said, "I guess it's a little more than just a coincidence they keep showing up. What do you guys think—shall we find out?"

Jesse turned to Rick and said, "I'm assuming since you just got off a plane, and by the way you're dressed, you didn't bring your gun with you, so I have an idea. Just keep walking to the truck as though we didn't notice them. Rick, do you remember what we did back in Saigon when you, me, and Danny were being followed by that ARVN (Army of the Republic of Vietnam) jeep?"

"I certainly do—how could I forget, my friend! Great idea," Rick replied.

Jesse was referring to an incident that took place while they were in Vietnam. You never knew who you could trust over there, unless it was one of your own people. With this in mind, whenever something seemed out of the ordinary, someone was acting suspicious, or you thought you were being watched or followed, you remedied the situation as soon as you could, so no one got hurt or killed. This had happened to Jesse, Rick, and their late friend Danny, and their quick action saved them. With that in mind, Jesse smirked, "Okay, you're behind the wheel, man without a gun, three men two guns," he smiled, winking at MJ.

The trio loaded into Jesse's big F-350 pickup and slowly began pulling out of the parking lot. Then in a blink of an eye, Rick floored the truck's accelerator pedal catapulting it right at the blue Blazer. At the last minute he made a quick turn, pulled the emergency brake and came to a sliding stop about six inches from the Blazer, blocking it from leaving. Jesse and MJ were out the door in a flash, one on each side of the Blazer, guns drawn and pointed in the window. Rick was standing on the running board of the pickup, with the 12 gauge shotgun Jesse kept behind the seat, loaded with .00 buckshot, pointed at the Blazers windshield.

Everything seemed to stand still for a moment. There appeared to be no sign of movement inside the vehicle. Jesse looked at MJ and nodded his head, simultaneously they pulled the doors open and jumped aside yelling "Get out! Get out!"

Nothing happened. No one got out. There were no occupants, the vehicle was empty.

"What in the hell is going on—is someone playing games with us?" MJ said to Jesse. Jesse stood there for a few minutes looking at the Blazer, deep in thought. "Well, guys I have a sneaky suspicion that the occupants of this fine vehicle are spooks," Jesse answered. Spooks is the term used for undercover operatives that spy on people or businesses. They could be looking for unusual or illegal activity or something specific, and reporting it back to whomever assigned them. Spooks are very common in government agencies with links to the CIA. They seem to appear out of nowhere. It's hard to distinguish them from anyone else. They act as though they have been there all along, and you just didn't notice them. Sometimes they stay around a while, other times they don't. Usually when they are satisfied with what they were trying to find out, they're gone as quickly as they arrived. Jesse and Rick were both familiar with this type of activity, having dealt with it in the military, particularly during their time in Vietnam. Whenever a suspicious person would arrive, they would joke amongst themselves about big brothers watching, or Bush is in the area, referring to George Bush Sr., who was previously head of the CIA, indicating a spook was there.

The trio searched the Blazer inside and out but were not surprised to find absolutely nothing—not a trace of the occupants or their belongings. This was also a good indication of who they were dealing with. Normal people, no matter how thorough they are about hiding their identity, often miss something, no matter how minute. Jesse, Rick, and MJ were not amateurs at this. They knew what they were doing and what to look for, but there was nothing to be found. That's what confirmed the indication—spooks—they were never there.

"Okay guys, let's call it a day and head to the campground," Jesse said. "I'm tired, hungry, and curious as hell about what's going on around here, and why someone's so interested in us."

It was just beginning to get dark and the lights along the roadway were beginning to shine in people's homes, casting a warm inviting glow. The sweet inviting smell of a wood fire, as families lit their wood stoves to take away the early chill, filled the air, as Jesse's F-350 pulled into the campground office parking area. "Home sweet home," Rick said with a sigh. "What surprises are you holding for us?"

The lights were on inside the recreation building, which was nothing more than a large extension of the office. There was a door separating the two areas that could be closed when necessary for privacy. The rec hall, as the building was referred to, was approximately fifty-foot square. It boasted a kitchen area with sinks, stoves, refrigerators, and freezers. There were two bathrooms, a shower, and a laundry area. The main hall had moveable tables, a large television, and a fireplace. There was a section with a small pool table and air-hockey game, shelves of books, board games and video games. Just about anything a person, group, or family would need for entertainment at camp. This also was the room where the person or persons that burgled the office had gained entrance.

Just as Jesse, MJ, and Rick got out of the truck, the hall door burst open and there was Katie with a big smile on her face, arms spread wide open, waiting in anticipation for hugs from her security force. "Thought you guys would never get here," she laughed. After many hugs and laughs, they all went inside.

"Wow!" Jesse exclaimed. "What did you do?" The room was all set up like a bunkhouse. There were three rollaway beds with extra linens and towels stacked on each one. In between the first two beds was a large wire cage with Neiko waiting anxiously to greet MJ, and there was the mouth-watering aroma of grilled ribs and chicken filling the air. "How did you know we all were coming?"

"Be serious Jesse," Katie answered. "Remember who you're talking to. I knew if one of you came, you would all come."

"I should have known all along, Katie. You know we appreciate it. This is perfect. Bear with us for a few minutes while we get our gear unpacked and settled in. I think we should mention a small encounter we had on our way up here. This whole thing, both incidents—the one here and then Doc's in Florida—have got to have a common denominator. I'm pretty convinced after this last encounter that your incident and Doc's are somehow connected. I'm just not sure how or why, but you can bet we're going to find out one way or another," Jesse replied.

After getting unpacked and relaxing for a while, everyone gathered around a rec hall table to enjoy a delicious sparerib and chicken wing dinner, with salad and French fries. The dinner had been prepared by Katie and her close friend Chloe, in anticipation of their arrival.

Chloe was the wife of Billy Murphy, Katie's chief of maintenance. She owned and operated her own catering service in the center of town. She, like her husband Billy, was well known and respected in the community. Whenever there was a function that needed a caterer, the person to call was Chole. When Chloe wasn't busy, she would drop by the campground and spend time with Katie, either visiting, or helping out with whatever needed to be done. She knew Katie was expecting Jesse, MJ, and Rick and offered to help Katie make dinner for the group. This certainly didn't hurt anyone's feelings or appetite—Chloe's cooking was the talk of the town. Rumor had it, although he won't admit it, that Jesse once commented, whenever you walked by food Chloe had prepared, it was as if the food called out your name, wanting you to try it.

After dinner was finished, the group shared all the information they had, concerning what now appeared to be three separate incidents. Jesse couldn't shake the feeling they may very well all be linked together in some way or another. Or was this just coincidence? Regardless, he was determined to find the answers and make sense of what was happening.

—11—

After coffee the next morning, Jesse asked Katie if anyone had checked out the rest of the campground for anything out of the ordinary since her office had been broken into, to which she answered she hadn't.

"Okay MJ," Jesse said, "why don't you and Rick give this place a quick going over and see if you find anything out of order or unusual. I'll run up to York and see our old friend Sheriff Eddie Bell, fill him in on the latest developments, and see if he has anything new for us. Keep me posted if you find anything. I should only be gone for a few hours."

Rick, MJ, and Neiko headed out to check out the campground. It was a cool sunshine-filled morning that would make their task a lot more enjoyable. They were equipped with notebooks and cameras so they could document anything that seemed out of place. They also took along walkie-talkies in order to keep in contact with each other, and with Katie at the office, if needed. The way things had been going lately, they didn't want to take any chances.

This was a large area to cover and to do it properly they decided to split up, each taking a section at a time. The camp was shaped similar to a horseshoe. If you were facing the open end of the horseshoe, campsites on the right side that were parallel to the outer fence line, were considered to be on the "A" side, and numbered to correspond with the side of the street they were on. For example, the first camp on the right side of the street was numbered A-1, while campsites on the opposite side of the street, the "B" side, began with B-1. This type of identifying and numbering continued throughout the camp, from street to street. MJ would take the "A" side while Rick would take the "B" side which bordered the interior, leaving the smaller areas such as "C," "D," "E," tent sites, and cabins, last. These areas were relatively small and they would do them together. A little over two hours went by and the two men completed both "A" and "B" sides of the camp with nothing unusual to report.

After a short coffee break, the search for abnormalities resumed, and they began checking the interior sites of the campground. The tent sites were just a quick walk-through, and the cabins were all secure and untouched. As they rounded the corner that led to "D" area, Rick stopped and said to MJ, "Hang on, I think the storm door on the last camp on the left is swinging open."

"You're right—stay alert," MJ answered. The pair slowly made their way to the camp with the swinging door.

"Hey, MJ," Rick said in a low voice, "this camp belongs to Doc and Peachy." The two men and Neiko slowly worked their way around the camp, each one taking a different side, checking for any open windows until they eventually met in the front, next to a small porch. Everything they checked up to this point was closed and appeared secured, with the exception of the front storm door, which was still swinging slowly in the slight breeze. "Maybe just blown open by the wind, but let's be sure," Rick said, as they cautiously made their way up on the front porch and tried the interior door. MJ turned the knob and pushed the door open, revealing a completely ransacked living area. There was also the faint smell of propane in the air.

"I just got a little whiff of gas—would you go check the tank and see if it might have been left on?" MJ asked, as he backed out the door of the camper. Rick ran around to the rear of the camper, found the gas tank, and sure enough the valve was all the way open. The gauge on the tank read empty, and the odor outside had dissipated. With this in mind, Rick was confident the danger of an explosion was over, and decided not to touch anything, hoping there might be fingerprints, or other telling evidence in the area.

MJ contacted Katie on his walkie-talkie and advised her that he and Rick had discovered a break-in at Doc and Peachy's camp. He asked her to call Jesse and let him know what he and Rick had found, and to see if Eddie Bell could send down a crew of crime scene investigators. He told her that although the campground was closed for the season, he and Rick would remain there and secure the scene. Both men were aware that permanent residents, with permission, were allowed to go to their respective campers. With that in mind, they wanted to check if someone passing by and saw the open door, didn't stop and attempt to close it. The smallest and most innocent thing that disturbs a crime scene quite often can have a serious impact on the investigation. MJ and Rick hoped to prevent that from happening.

Just shortly after lunch time, Jesse's big F-350 pulled up the street followed by a York County sheriff's crime scene van with three deputies inside. After brief introductions, MJ and Rick filled the deputies in on what they had discovered. They also reassured them that no one had been near the property since their arrival. The deputies thanked them, said they would talk later, and began their investigation.

Knowing it would take a good part of the afternoon for the crime scene crew to finish, Jesse, MJ, and Rick decided they would go back to the rec hall and await the outcome of the deputies' investigation. This would also give them a chance to toss around ideas on what was going on, have some lunch, and give MJ time to feed Neiko.

Neiko, unlike most dogs or pets, did not have a specific feeding schedule. He was fed out of MJ's hand, and that only occurred when he was specifically doing his job, finding electronics. In order for him to perform at his best, he had to be a little hungry, and the possibility of him being called out at any time would not work if he had a set schedule to eat. MJ would place electronics in various places and have Neiko find them at odd hours of the day, thus feeding him and keeping him alert to his duties. MJ decided he would place a few flash drives and cellphones around the outside of the rec hall and the vehicles parked there, and put Neiko to work. MJ and Neiko began their usual routine and within a short period of time, Neiko had found all the hidden objects, as he always did. Just as MJ started to gather up his training gear and go back inside the building, Neiko stopped at the rear of Jesses' truck, turned, and sat by the rear bumper.

"What have you got, Neiko? Show me," MJ said. Neiko put his head under the spare tire holder of the truck and made a noise with his nose. MJ got down on his knees and crawled under the truck, looking in the area Neiko was indicating. After a few minutes he crawled back out with a smile on his face. "Hey guys, isn't this interesting?" he said with a grin, holding up a small tracking device in his hand.

"Well, I'll be damned," Jesse said, as he shook his head in disgust, no wonder our friends in the blue Blazer were able to drop out of sight, but keep tabs on our location. Well guys, I guess that makes it pretty obvious we're also involved in this mess, for some reason or another. I think we should put that thing back MJ. Maybe we can catch them at their own game. You might as well have Neiko check Katie's and Chloe's cars while we're right here." After a thorough check of Katie's and Chloe's cars, which turned up nothing, they all went back inside to wait for any information the crime scene investigators may have to share with them.

When investigators are working a case, sometimes things just seem to fall into place, and the outcome is exactly what you had expected. Then there's the occasions where questions lead to questions and more questions, and frustration can take over. You know you're right, but just can't seem to put it all together. So you go back and begin to check and double-check yourself. Then out of nowhere, someone says something and bingo, there's the answer. You were right all along and the obvious is looking you right in the face. Jesse concluded that this might be one of those occasions. He then proceeded to tell Rick, MJ, and Katie about his conversation with Sheriff Eddie Bell regarding the office break-in, and the blue Blazer incident.

Eddie, laughingly, reminded Jesse that sometimes you can't see the forest for the trees. "I've been giving it some serious thought since you first called me, putting all these incidents together. Here's what I think. First you have Katie's break-in, next Doc's incident, and then all of a sudden you guys are being followed. I would be willing to bet the break-in was to find Doc's address in Florida for reasons unknown. It would be obvious to whomever broke in that you, Jesse, being chief of security, would be notified. Then take into account you three, along with Doc, have been involved in numerous investigations together, ranging from stolen campers, holes in the lower fence, someone flying a drone over the camp taking pictures, and a missing girl. Correct me if I'm wrong, but each time these incidents took place not just one of you got involved—you all got involved. Putting all this info together, it would appear to me that someone is definitely after Doc, for reasons unknown. Keeping that in mind I think, whoever it is, they want to see if you three are going to do the usual, and also get involved. You guys are like the three amigos. If one's in, you're all in. Oh, and don't be surprised if you find a tracker on MJ's truck when you return to pick it up, and I'd be willing to bet someone was tailing Rick from Arizona as well."

Just as Jesse finished explaining what Eddie Bell had said, the crime scene investigators came into the rec hall, shaking their heads. They had little information to share that was of any value. All they could definitely say was that the intruders appeared to have worn gloves and covered their shoes. The place was totally ransacked, drawers opened and dumped, cabinets torn off the wall, mattresses and rugs cut and pulled apart—even pictures taken off the walls and cut open. On top of all this all the gas stove burners were turned to the on position, with no flame, hoping to fill the camp with gas, just waiting for some kind of ignition to blow it up.

"There's no question someone was looking for something important to them," the lead investigator said. "And of course, there's doesn't appear to be any way to tell if they found what they were after. We'll be filing a full report when we get back to the office. It will be ready in a day or two. Looks like whoever did this are real professionals. Haven't seen anything like this in quite a while. I'd watch my back if I were you."

Jesse thanked them and said he'd give Eddie a call in a few days. "Well guys, I think we better have a talk with our friend Doc, real soon."

* * *

Sunshine was making a brave attempt to hold back the late fall evening clouds, and the familiar smell of smoke from wood stoves was beginning to fill the cool late afternoon air. Jesse had been on the phone for the past hour or so, trying to reach Doc and Peachy in Florida, but to no avail. Rick, MJ, and Katie were going over as many scenarios as they could, trying to piece together whatever was going on. It was like playing connect the dots, using what little information they had.

Since it was beginning to get dark, it was decided the best time to check Doc's camp again would be first thing in the morning. Poking around in the dark was not a productive use of their time, particularly when they had no idea what they were looking for.

Even though a team of crime scene investigators didn't find anything of significance regarding the reason for the break-in, at this point they could only speculate until further investigation could be done. Their main purpose at this point in time was to record and document what they found at the scene. With any luck, Jesse would make contact with Doc before morning and see if there was any more information that could be passed on to the sheriff's office.

* * *

Night fell and darkness enveloped Happy Valley. There was a full moon making its way up in the crystal clear sky adding to the beauty of this picture-book campground. Katie had returned home to get some much needed rest. She had been busy the last few days getting things ready for the guys to arrive. Jesse, Rick, and MJ—or the three amigos—as Eddie Bell jokingly called them, were sitting around the rec hall sipping cold beers and swapping ideas on where to start in the morning. Jesse made several more attempts to reach Doc but was unable to make contact and suggested they call it a night.

"You guys go to bed. I'm going to take Neiko outside for a quick walk and I'll lock up when I come in," MJ said, as he stepped outside and closed the door. Jesse and Rick decided to have another beer and wait for MJ's return. The pair sat and drank their beers, bouncing questions about the case off each other, when Jesse said to Rick, "This is strange—what do you suppose is taking MJ so long?"

"You're right, it has been quite a while. Think we should go take a look?" No sooner had Rick finished asking about going to look for MJ, than the door of the rec hall burst open and Neiko followed by a puzzled-looking MJ came in. He walked straight through the rec hall, opened the door that led to the office, stepped into the dark room and looked out the window.

"What's going on?" Jesse asked, as he and Rick followed MJ into the darkened room.

"I thought all the power in the camp area was turned off for the winter," MJ replied, as he continued to look out into the darkness.

"It is," Jesse answered. "The only power not turned off is the rec hall and office area, in order to allow for everyday operations."

"Well then listen to this. When I went out with Neiko, we walked up by the pool area just to take a better look at the full moon. We had just turned the corner by the pump house when I thought I saw a light down by Gossip Valley. We sat out there awhile looking and watching but nothing happened. Then just as we started to come inside, sure enough I saw it again. At first I thought it was a reflection from a car or something, but there's no traffic at all. At least nothing remotely close to the campground, never mind down in Gossip Valley.

"Well I'll be damned, it appears the plot thickens my friends. Looks like our work is cut out for us tomorrow," Jesse said.

At that very moment, with excitement in his voice, Rick said, "Hey there's your light, MJ, left side of the hill." The three watched the light disappear as quickly as it appeared.

"You're right, MJ, that's no reflection. There's no question, it's a light and it appeared to be moving slowly, but to where?" Jesse wondered. "There's no camps around that area, unless Billy Murphy is putting something together down there that he's going to pull up when he's finished with it. He does that kind of stuff now and then to keep the clutter out of the camp area and it gives him easy access to the dump when he uses the big truck." Billy was not only chief of maintenance but he also did remodeling on the camps during the off season. "We can check with him in the morning before we go down there, but why would someone be there in the dark?"

"Maybe you're right, someone's stealing stuff, but there is

one other thing that comes to mind," Rick said. "What about the bunker?"

"The bunker," Jesse and MJ said almost simultaneously. "Don't even suggest that crap is happening again," Jesse grumbled. Rick was referring to the bunker built down on the side of the campground hill where all the drainage pipes were connected. The bunker was a perfectly-hidden concrete shelter built into the hillside. This was where Howie Wang's helpers would bring the young women they were trafficking, give them new clothes, and sell them for a nice profit. It was also the spot where Doc was wounded in a shootout with Howie, when Doc attempted to free the women. In the end, all turned out well—the women were rescued, Howie and two of his accomplices were fatally shot, and the others involved in the trafficking ring were arrested. "You know we're going down there in the morning after we talk to Billy," Jesse remarked. "I hate this shit. We need to find Doc."

The three men sat in the darkened room together for another hour, waiting and looking, but didn't see the light again. "Let's turn in and hit it hard in the morning guys," Jesse finally said.

—12—

The trio went to bed and slept the few short hours left until dawn, then they were up making a plan for the day. Jesse tried calling Doc again but to no avail. There was still no answer on his or Peachy's phone.

"I don't like this guys, something must be wrong. Where the hell are they?" Jesse growled. "Hey, MJ, you don't suppose any of our predictably wayward friends, could be down south on forced vacation, do you? Maybe they could do a little checking for us if they are." The friends Jesse was referring to, were a small group of individuals that seemed to think that law and order did not pertain to them. Jesse has had occasion to deal with these characters more than once. They are not exactly the type of people you would have over for dinner. Some of their exploits, although not all proven, range from every crime you can think of, beginning with simple assault. If you can name it, they have either done it or have probably been involved in one way or another. They are considered by most people to be very dangerous, but for some reason they liked helping Jesse, MJ, and Rick. One might call it a relationship out of mutual respect—mainly because they knew the trio also had a reputation of being dangerous, if necessary.

"Great idea! I'll start making calls and find out," MJ said.

"Listen, MJ, we just want them to look around and tell us what they find. None of their other nonsense, if you know what I mean," Jesse said, shaking his head and laughing.

"Oh boy, here we go," said Rick laughing. "We're putting a fox in the hen house and saying be a good boy."

"Before you give one of them the word, MJ, let me know who's down there, we better be a little careful," Jesse said with a smirk on his face.

Katie arrived bright and early with fresh coffee and donuts and while the group ate, Jesse filled her in on the lights that they had seen in the field during the night. "Oh no, not again," Katie mumbled.

"Yeah, it looks like it. We're going to go down below shortly and have a look around. It may be absolutely nothing—or maybe someone checking out Billy's building material, but we have to find out for sure. If you're going to be here in the office for the rest of the day, I want you to go home and get that .38 cal. Lady Smith revolver David gave you, if you don't already have it in your purse, and keep it close by. I also think you should lock the back door while you're alone in here, at least until we find out exactly what's going on," Jesse replied.

After finishing their coffee the three amigos stepped out the rear side door of the rec hall and listened for the lock to engage before heading to the lower section of the campground. They slowly and methodically worked their way throughout the lower section of the campground into the area referred to as Gossip Valley. This was the area where the light they had seen during the night appeared to be coming from. They made their way through the area looking for anything that might appear out of place, but found nothing.

"Let's cut back through the drain area and check out the bunker while we're here," Rick said. "It might be a waste of time, but who knows, that light came from somewhere."

Jesse and MJ both agreed, and they wove their way up the embankment through the drain area to the bunker. As they approached the drain leading to the bunker, they noticed the grass appeared trodden down, and there were a few fresh tracks in the mud. There was no question someone had been there recently.

When they got to the door, they found the outside lock had been cut off, and the door was ajar. Jesse and Rick entered the bunker with caution, while MJ stood watch in the tunnel entrance.

"Bingo," Jesse said. The inside of the bunker had been trashed. What little had been left behind after the investigation was strewn everywhere.

"Wow, someone's really looking for something! You figure it's the same ones that were at Doc's place?" Rick asked, shaking his head.

"I'd bet on it," Jesse answered. "Let's take a quick look around, lock this place back up, then go back to the office and think."

After returning to the rec hall, they all sat around bouncing questions and answers off each other hoping to come up with some reason for the latest events. Why would someone want Doc's address in Florida, then put a gun in his face? Why trash his camp here in Maine? What were they looking for in the bunker? Why were Rick, MJ, and Jesse being followed?

"You don't think it could have anything to do with that episode we had last summer, regarding Howie and his bunch, do you?" Katie asked.

"I think it has everything to do with it, but I can't figure out what. Any ideas?" Jesse asked. "I wish we could find Doc and maybe get some answers. Did you hear anything back from our friends, MJ?"

"Actually we hit the jackpot, it seems there was some kind of event taking place in Boston last week that didn't turn out as expected. By the time the event was over the building was filled with smoke, there were several gunshots and an unidentified person fell or was pushed down a flight of stairs during the chaos. Police have refused to comment or to elaborate on the situation as of yet. It appears no one was killed, just minor injuries were reported. Strange thing is, shortly after the incident, three of our friends were seen boarding the midnight Amtrak to Florida. Do you think they just wanted to see a little spring training? Baseball camp is open, you know," MJ replied with a chuckle.

"No doubt in my mind—they're big sports fans and wouldn't miss spring training for the world. It's pretty obvious from what you told me who it is. See if you can reach out to them. Ask them to try and be as inconspicuous as possible. Oh and MJ, you can also tell them we owe them one—as though they won't remind us," Jesse answered.

"Okay, I'll send Hawkeye a text with the address right now," MJ said.

* * *

The rest of the afternoon was spent on routine investigations—phone calls, question and answer sessions on the whats and what ifs, and more phone calls. Jesse left to visit Sheriff Eddie Bell to see if there was anything new concerning the break-in at Doc's camp and fill him in on the bunker being ransacked. MJ and Rick decided to go back to Doc's camp and do little looking around themselves, just in case. They also wanted to make sure it was secure.

The late fall skies were threatening as they made their way back to the rec hall and the damp fog was rolling in from the ocean, putting a little chill in the air. Just as they arrived back at the hall, Jesse was returning from the sheriff's office, where he had hoped to get some new information on the investigation.

"Well, that was a waste of time, guys," he quipped. "Eddie was in full agreement with his investigators, that whoever trashed Doc's place were professionals and left nothing behind to connect them. All we can do for now is wait and hope our friends down south come up with something that will help us out. So on that note, I say we have a drink and something to eat. Katie made a big beef stew with biscuits."

After finishing off Katie's wonderful beef stew and biscuits, Rick suggested they make an evening sweep of the campground before calling it a night, in hope of seeing someone or something out of the ordinary. Everyone agreed that it was better than just sitting and waiting. As they started out the door, MJ's cell phone beeped indicating there was a new message waiting. MJ read the message, started laughing, and held the phone up for Rick and Jesse to see. The message read: this is a burner phone I'm using. Go buy a burner and call me at this number, your friend, John Doe.

Jesse shook his head laughing, "That damn Hawkeye, he's definitely a piece of work. Let's go to town and get a phone." A burner phone is a cheap prepaid phone that can be purchased at almost any department or convenience store. Usually people buy them to hide their identification or avoid having their calls traced or connected to them in any way. They usually pay cash for them, to avoid any paper trail and throw them away after they use them.

It was getting late, so the trio headed into town. As luck would have it, they found one at a local WalMart, picked up a few supplies, and headed back to camp. After settling in again at camp, Jesse put in a call to the number Hawkeye had texted from. The conversation was brief, as were all conversations with Hawkeye. Jesse ended the call and sat looking out the window, rubbing the knee he had been shot in. This was a habit he had when he was thinking, or trying to figure something out.

Finally, he looked at the others, shaking his head, "You won't believe this," he said. "Hawkeye told me that he and Giggles went to Doc's place pretending to be pest control people sent by the condominium association to see if there were any complaints about bugs. They had already gone to other buildings just to make it look legitimate in case they were being watched. Hawkeye said a man and lady answered the door, introducing themselves as Doc and Peachy. They said they had no bug complaints but thanked the men for coming. When they got back to the truck they borrowed, or claimed to have borrowed, Diamond Dave was sitting behind the wheel shaking his head. He told Hawkeye he recognized the guy at the door as a federal agent that had been tailing him a few years back in regards to a fire bombing incident that he denies having anything to do with. Hawkeye told him they claimed to be Doc and Peachy but Diamond Dave said that's not possible, and he was positive who it was. I don't like this at all," Jesse said.

—13—

The following morning the sun was rising as the coffee was brewing and the bacon was smelling like a little bit of heaven in the pan. The three amigos were just sitting down to eat when there was a sharp rap on the door. They exchanged a quick look, and then instinctively positioned themselves in different parts of the room. They knew it wouldn't be Katie, Billy, or Chloe, since they all had a key and would not knock. With that in mind, they felt it best to be over-cautious, particularly the way things had been going thus far. Jesse made eye contact with the others, nodded then quickly stepped aside as he opened the door. In stepped four well-dressed men and a woman. They were all holding up wallets showing badges and identification cards that read in large letters: FBI.

The first person through the door was a very large man with a movie star smile and a booming voice. "Good morning, gentlemen, we're with the Federal Bureau of Investigation. I'm Agent Smith and these are agents Jones, Johnson, Hill, and Gray. Did we miss breakfast?" he asked with a grin.

"By no means, there's plenty for all. What can we do for you, besides feed you?" Jesse smiled right back.

"First of all," Agent Smith replied, "I believe it's time we got this matter regarding one of our agents, the one you call Doc, cleared up. By doing this, maybe we can bring closure to our case and all return to our normal everyday activities. May we sit down?"

"By all means, sit down and have some breakfast while it's

still hot, and rest assured we're all ears to know what you consider to be normal activities," Jesse smiled.

"That's what I was hoping you would say," Agent Smith replied. "To start with, we all know you people are here because you believe your friend, Doc, is in some kind of trouble. We hope to help you put those fears to rest. I can assure you he is fine. Unfortunately, you won't be able to talk with him at the present time. He's out of the country on assignment. I can't say for sure, because of security reasons, as you must understand. With that being said, let me compliment you on the way your friends in Florida handled themselves when they came to his condominium, looking for him and Agent Keene. Agents Jones and Johnson, over there," he said, pointing to one of the other men and the woman sitting at the end of the table, with big smiles on their face, are the ones that answered the door.

"They recognized the driver of the pest control van, as our old friend Diamond Dave. We had him under surveillance several years ago in regards to a US Post Office fire. I still personally think he did it, but regardless, we couldn't prove it, at least not yet," Agent Smith continued. "Now let me explain exactly what caused the other problems we have had, such as the break-in here at the campground and the gun incident in Florida. I'm sure you remember the trafficking case you were all involved in, but you may not be aware there were a few repercussions we didn't expect.

"It seems someone else here at the campground that we all were unaware of, was also involved. His identity was only known to us as Mr. Wang. This person had pretended to be good friends with Doc. He knew Doc was an agent so he tried to stay close, hoping to have an inside track, if Doc were to reveal any information concerning the trafficking ring. The only problem with his plan was that Doc had no idea the ring existed until after the missing girl incident. So in actuality, he was wasting his time. Soon after the ring incident was resolved and we considered the case closed, it was abruptly reopened. It seems the word got out that someone had found and taken a list containing the names of some pretty high government officials, senators, and congressmen, that were somehow involved in or aware of the trafficking. Without question it was assumed the lead agents on the case were the most likely to have the list. The agents were Smith and Keene, or Doc and Peachy, as you refer to them. Subsequently some highly-qualified former undercover government operatives were recruited, and put to the task of finding the list before some pretty important heads rolled," Agent Smith paused for a moment, then continued.

"This brings us to the break-in here at the campground. That was carried out by a female relative of that same person that had befriended Doc for information. The relative wanted Doc's Florida address, as you figured out right away. You also probably know by now, who the friend was. You had a lead earlier in the case, thanks to Katie's quick thinking with the license plate photo. Unfortunately, when you saw who the license plate belonged to, you didn't believe it. When the relative contacted him and advised him of what had transpired here at the campground, and how she almost got caught, he panicked. Through his own experience, he figured Katie would have taken the plate number and expected her to call you people.

"Realizing what could happen after you were contacted and the problems it would cause, he let the other ring members know. That's when they started watching and following you. These people are also the same ones responsible for the break-in at Doc's camp and the bunker being ransacked, while looking for the list. There's no telling what they may have done next—they have no limits. Fortunately, they have all been rounded up by US Marshalls, including your friend Eugene (Rocky) Campbell in Florida, and are behind bars. The justice department will handle the government higher ups once we get the list of names from you, Mr. McGrath," Agent Smith concluded.

"What the hell are you talking about? I don't have any list of names," Jesse stammered.

"You do, but just don't know it," Agent Smith laughed. "Doc said I should tell you to go get his favorite bottle of Captain Morgan Spiced Rum—the one he had given to you for safekeeping when he left."

Jesse just shook his head as he went into the security closet and returned with the bottle of Captain Morgan Spiced Rum, as Agent Smith requested. "Doc said he trusted you completely and that he knew the list would be safe with you. Now carefully peel the large label off the face of the bottle and let's see what's there."

Jesse peeled the label off carefully and out fell a small piece of white paper with several names written on it.

"Holy shit!" MJ and Rick said simultaneously.

"Well gentlemen that just about wraps it up," Agent Smith said with a big grin. "I think as long as you have that bottle out here we all should have a toast to Agents Smith and Keene, or is it Doc and Peachy?" he asked.

Just then the door opened and in walked Katie, with a surprised look on her face. "Wow, what did I miss?" she asked. "Come on and have a seat, Katie. We have a story to tell you. Maybe you should have a drink first. I hope the ghost is listening," Jesse laughed. Then everyone at the table burst out laughing.

There was an obvious sense of relief throughout the room as Jesse and the FBI agents explained to Katie what they had concluded regarding the campground break-in, and the problem Doc had encountered in Florida. It was apparent that everyone had the same relieved feeling. They were all laughing and joking as if a heavy weight had been lifted off their shoulders. That is, all except for Jesse. He had been doing this kind of work for almost half of his adult life, and for some reason he had that familiar feeling, something wasn't right about the conclusion. Maybe it's just because the FBI agents were being so open and friendly. That in itself was strange. They were infamous for showing up when the real investigative work was over and then grandstanding to take all the credit. Actually, that's not necessarily true for all the agents. The bureau has many top-notch investigators, but as in every profession, there's always a few attention grabbers, or as Jesse refers to them—the losers. The overly-friendly working-together-attitude the agents had, was enough to make Jesse more than a little suspicious. He had a feeling there was something else going on, but just wasn't sure what. *Oh well,* he thought to himself, *better not to look a gift horse in the mouth, I can't let my doubts and suspicions ruin the moment for everyone else.* Although at the same time he was also thinking, *these guys are full of it, what's really going on, and where the hell are Doc and Peachy?*

* * *

Late afternoon rolled around, the sky began to darken and the wind was beginning to blow in some cold fall air. Smoke from wood stoves began to fill the crisp air. The festivities had come to an end. The FBI agents said their fond farewells with phony promises, handshakes, and smiles, then left for who knows where. Jesse, Rick, MJ and Katie sat around discussing the events of the day with disbelief.

"Okay Jesse, tell us what you think," Rick said. "We know you didn't buy that FBI dog and pony show. Neither did we."

Jesse nodded his with a smile on his face. "This is scary. You guys are as suspicious as I am about our gracious fellow investigators and their intentions. Does anyone have any ideas, thoughts, or anything concerning this visit? Personally, I wouldn't trust that bunch as far as I could throw them, nor do I believe a single thing they said. The only thing that bothers me is the note behind the Captain Morgan label, that's definitely a Doc idea. Except for that, in my opinion, everything else they said was all a bunch of bull if you know what I mean."

"Well guys, it looks like we have a few things to discuss, Katie said why don't I get a hot dinner going. It's getting cold outside and we may be here awhile."

"Great idea, Katie," MJ replied. "I have to feed Neiko anyway, so this is as good a time as any." Katie went into the kitchen area and started meal preparations. Jesse and Rick sat back, cracked a cold beer and watched MJ hide electronics for Neiko to find. It was almost impossible to outsmart that dog. When MJ had all the electronics hidden, he put Neiko through the usual routine they do before they start each search, then on command Neiko began searching. They had just started around the room when Neiko stopped at a location where MJ had not hidden anything, and was indicating he had found something. MJ gave Jesse and Rick a questioning look, then checked the area, to see what Neiko had found. Nodding his head and smiling, he turned toward the others, and put his fingers to his lips prompting Jesse and Rick to stop talking. Then MJ pointed to a small Bingo scoring board hanging by the exit door that had gotten Neiko's attention. Jesse and Rick understood that MJ was indicating there was something, most likely a listening device, planted on the sign. "Let's go up front, see if Katie needs any help with dinner," Jesse said to Rick. "It will be a while before MJ's done."

Once in the front office, they closed the door and told Katie that MJ found some sort of listening device, likely left behind by their FBI friends. "I'm not one bit surprised, coming from that bunch," Katie responded. "David used to say, never trust those FBI suits with all their smiles as far as you can throw them. But what the hell do you suppose is going on?"

Jesse and Rick shook their heads, opened a beer, and sat down and looked at her. "I'm afraid that's what we're going to have to find out by ourselves. That pack of phonies that just paid us a visit certainly had no intention of helping us. Here's what I think we should do," Jesse said. "Let's leave their listening device where it is and pretend we believed them. All real conversations concerning Doc and Peachy will take place either outside of the building or here in the front office. In the meantime, let's all have something to eat. After that we start at the very beginning and talk this thing through, maybe we missed something. While you guys are in here tossing things around, maybe you could make up a facts board. I'm going to try and think like Doc, and start with the booze bottles in the security locker. He might have been sending us a message in his own secret way, if you know what I mean."

After a hearty dinner had been devoured and the pans and dishes cleared away, the group got down to business. They tossed around and put in order everything they could think of, no matter how insignificant it seemed, regarding the events that had transpired since the campground break-ins and Doc's problem. Only things they could verify were marked on the fact board, as they formed a timeline for the chain of events. Everything else would be put aside and saved for future reference. It was a long, tedious evening for all, as they tried to be precise on the chain of events and when they had occurred.

Just as they were finishing up, Jesse burst through the door from the security locker room with a big smile on his face. "Relax, guys I found what we needed, it's all here. That damn Doc, he is a genius. Remember our 'new friend Agent Smith' telling us to look behind the label of Doc's favorite bottle of Captain Morgan spiced rum? Well I kept thinking about it and then it came to me. Captain Morgan was not Doc's favorite drink—that was Peachy's. The good doctor's favorite drink was Grey Goose vodka. So I went through the security locker and way in the back, behind the old walkie-talkies, found a bottle of Grey Goose. I peeled the label back just like I did on the Captain Morgan bottle and bingo! This fell out," he said, as he held up a small white piece of paper. The paper said: *Jesse, get your shotgun out of your truck, look closely at the shells you have on the butt stock carrier.*

Jesse went to the truck and brought his shotgun inside. He examined the shells as instructed and found one of them had been cut open, the powder removed, and a neatly rolled piece of paper tightly wrapped in plastic wrap. Jesse carefully removed the wrap, revealing a typewritten note, and straightened it out, being careful not to tear it. "Okay guys, if you're ready, I'll read this out loud, maybe it will explain a few things.

> *If you are reading this, Agent Smith has been there, and you realized after he left, that the Captain Morgan's was Peachy's—not mine—I hoped you would eventually figure that out and look for my Grey Goose! Good job! Agent Smith is a real good guy and can be trusted. The list of names you found under the Captain Morgan's label and gave to him had all the names except one. The name missing from the list is someone who may be in the pocket of the traffickers. When I get back, I will give that name privately to Agent Smith. I couldn't take the chance of revealing the name, not knowing who would be present if Agent Smith did come to see you. Peachy and I are okay and we'll see you soon! Don't forget we have a wedding coming up!*

When Jesse finished reading Doc's note, he looked up and saw a roomful of smiling faces. You could sense the feeling of relief.

"Well my friends, I guess that just about wraps this mess up. It was without question a team effort and I am personally damned proud to be a member of the team. It appears Doc and Peachy are alive and well so all I can say is thank you for everything. Let's go home. I have a feeling snow will be arriving soon. See you in the spring!"

~ Part 3 ~

—14—

Just as Jesse predicted, winter arrived in all its fury bringing with it three solid months of wind, snow, and bitter cold. Finally with very little fan-fair, it slowly departed, giving way to blue skies and sunshine. Once again it was time for Jesse to go back to Happy Valley and prepare to open for the season.

The opening went without a hitch and the season went into full swing as usual. It turned out to be a relatively quiet year at camp. It seems to hold true for any other business or activity, some years can be hectic and some just quiet and peaceful. Jesse preferred the quiet ones. Now things are being wrapped up for the summer, the campers and seasonal residents have all left for their respective winter destination and the staff is once again saying goodbye until next year.

* * *

Jesse arrived back at his hunting camp, where the fall season was in full swing. Mother Nature had been busy working her magic and changing the scenery. A light dusting of snow was beginning to appear on the high mountain peaks. The air was cold and fresh with just a little bite to it. The ski areas were beginning to come alive and gear up in anticipation for another season. The sounds of the snow grooming machines coming to life and being tested after being silent during the long summer, could be heard in the distance. You can imagine the hustle and bustle of the ski technicians and lift mechanics, as they began swarming like ants, checking the chairs, tow ropes, and lift cables for safety. What a busy, happy time in ski country.

Jesse loved the changing of the seasons along with the cold and the snow that would soon be arriving. Above all though, there was one tradition that's lasted for the past twenty years or more. A group of friends he works with at the campground in Maine, where he is chief of security, come to visit his white mountain retreat. They usually spend a week or so, at this picture-perfect camp, hunting, drinking, relaxing, and telling tall tales. Jesse has added onto the structure in the last few years. It now boasts a huge bunkhouse with four bedrooms, two baths and a full kitchen. This new addition is mainly used during hunting season or when any of these close friends needed to get away. Strangers are not welcome. The bunkhouse is connected to the main cabin and can only be entered from there. This is where Jesse and his friends wind down whenever they want or need to.

MJ Davis is usually the first one at camp. He still works for the task force, investigating internet crimes against children. Usually by this time of year he's ready for a break and welcomes his chance to get away. Too bad he isn't as good a hunter as he is drinker and talker, Jesse would often quip.

Then there's Doc and Rick. They usually arrive a little later, due to the fact they have to travel from their winter hideaway. You are never really sure where these guys could be. Doc is usually at his condo in Florida, unless he's off on some kind of secret squirrel stuff for the government. Rick could be anywhere that it's warm, so long as he can play golf. Regardless of where any member of this group may be, hunting camp has become a priority to all of them, and they always come. Doc likes to think he can talk the deer into giving up or negotiate a deal. If not, he threatens to make a call. Therefore he doesn't worry about getting into the woods too early. Rick, on the other hand, is a very good hunter. He's usually out in the woods before anyone, and on the flip side, returns before anyone. Most likely on his return, you can find him looking like a seagull, in search of cold beer and leftover spare ribs, which are cooked almost daily at camp.

On a few occasions Billy Murphy, the Happy Valley maintenance chief, Docs' girlfriend Peachy and even sheriff Eddie Bell, from York County, Maine, have come and joined the happy group. Billy Murphy has the same attitude when he's hunting as he does at work. It can either be the easy way or the hard way. If he has to go after the deer, they better look out. Peachy, on the other hand, is a crack shot but doesn't let on, unless she is challenged and it involves a money pool. Eddie Bell is also a crack shot, kind of laid back but relentless. He could probably kill the deer with his bare hands. This man is really big. What a great bunch, Jesse thought.

Unfortunately, this year would not be like other years and it may never be the same for this tight-knit group. Jesse was standing on the front porch of his camp, looking out at the majestic mountains he loved so much, asking himself, why did this have to happen to us? His mind constantly racing back to the unbelievable series of events that had previously turned a major part of his—and the campground family's world—upside down.

—15—

It was all set, a command decision had been made—Doc and Peachy were finally going to tie the knot. They decided after all these years of being together, traveling halfway around the world—sharing some good and some very dangerous times—they were meant to be together. They set a date in September, so they could enjoy a short honeymoon before joining the rest of the group at Jesse's for the annual hunting camp ritual. It would be like a storybook wedding. This couple has been through hell and high water together. From internal government affairs and investigations to being on the front lines fighting in countries that can't be mentioned, because they were never there, according to the government. Without question, with these two finally married, this was looking like the best hunting camp season ever. No cases to work on or phones to answer—just one good time for all.

Well, as fate would have it, things didn't turn out exactly as planned. In only a few short minutes, time seemed to stop, dealing an irreversible blow to all concerned.

* * *

It was September 21st, a beautiful cool sunny day, not a cloud in the sky. The jovial wedding party was gathered at the hall entrance. You could feel the excitement as you watched them. There were smiles, giggles, back slaps and high-fives exchanged. It was almost contagious. This was definitely a special day for two really special people. What more could one ask for?

The bride, Peachy, was as radiant as ever, smiling and

laughing as she watched her friends and family enjoying themselves. Only a few close friends were aware that this kind, friendly girl living next door, was actually a fierce and deadly undercover agent. Then there was the groom, Doc, with his ho-hum, never worry attitude, also another deadly undercover operative, just being Doc.

When the wedding introduction music began to play, a hush fell over the crowd in anxious anticipation of the bride and groom's appearance. Suddenly, like a page out of a Stephen King novel, all hell broke loose. The quiet, happy atmosphere turned into turmoil. The staccato of automatic weapon fire filled the air, sending everyone chaotically scurrying for shelter. That is, everyone except Doc and Peachy. When the shooting stopped, they were found lying in the center aisle, arms wrapped around each other, covered with blood. People rushed for the door, screaming and crying. Rick recognized the familiar sound of gunfire too well. There was a time back in Vietnam when it was a way of life for him and Jesse. No matter how hard you try, there's some things you never forget.

Rick instinctively yelled, "Everyone get down! Someone call 911!" as he rushed in wild abandon to Doc and Peachy's sides.

Jesse and MJ knelt there, next to their friends, guns drawn and looking in every direction for the shooter. In what seemed like hours, but was actually only minutes, police, fire, and sheriff deputies were on the scene. While the EMTs were tending to the wounded, the deputies and police, along with Jesse, Rick, and MJ, began searching for the shooter and securing the area. The search was quick and thorough, but to no avail, the shooter or shooters were long gone, without leaving a trace.

After a speedy evaluation by the EMTs, Doc and Peachy were placed into ambulances and transported to the emergency hospital.

Peachy was treated for multiple gunshot wounds. She was

evaluated as in critical but stable condition, and put into an ICU with police security outside her door. Doc, on the other hand, was not as fortunate, and to the shock and disbelief of all those present, was pronounced dead. A sheet was pulled up over his head, and the blood-spattered gurney he was lying on was wheeled down the hall to a waiting area. The quiet in the room was almost deafening, as those in attendance were beginning to come to terms with what had just transpired.

Then almost on cue, the quiet was disrupted, and more confusion ensued, as the second most bizarre incident of the day began to unfold. Several federal agents appeared in the hospital lobby. Of course, they entered in their "more-powerful-than-thee" fashion. They were all wearing black trench coats, fashion magazine sunglasses, and earphones, swarming around like a bunch of black bugs. This typical grand entrance was also accompanied by the flashing of their ID cards as they announced, "FBI—everyone stand back."

As Jesse watched, all he could think to himself was *oh boy, just what we needed, here come the mental midgets*. The agents were taking turns having words with the doctors at the front desk, each trying to outdo the other, with their "I said-he said" routine. To everyone's amazement except Jesse's (he'd seen this act before), the agents wheeled Doc's gurney to a waiting van. They quickly loaded it inside, and left the hospital grounds. No one in attendance could quite comprehend what had just taken place or why, so with heavy hearts they went their separate ways, bewildered by what had just transpired.

—16—

Two long months later, Jesse was sitting on his hunting camp porch having an early morning coffee. His thoughts were on Peachy recovering from her wounds, at least physically, that is. Jesse knew she was an emotional wreck, and with good reason. He was hoping she would come to camp and relax. Family needs family at times like this, even if it's just for a short period. This group of men and women have all worked together for many years. They have been through both very good times and very dangerous ones, always managing to prevail.

This might be a good time, Jesse thought, to put in a call to Peppermint Patty—his favorite psychologist. Jesse and Patty have been friends for years and she has always been willing to help whenever Jesse asked. He had contacted her for assistance with a case he was working on a few years earlier involving a young girl named Susan. On that particular occasion, Patty responded without hesitation and worked her mental magic. He's now considering inviting Patty to hunting camp, hoping she could talk to Peachy and help heal her emotional pain. It certainly couldn't hurt.

* * *

Jesse wiped his eyes and decided to do a little scouting. It was a perfect day to take a look around. The air was crisp and clear and calm. He thought this would be a good time to look for some rubs or scrapes, as he made his way into the tree line. Scrapes and rubs are distinctive marks that deer make on the ground and on trees to communicate with other deer. This is a way of marking their territory and also indicating they are ready to breed.

He had decided not to take his rifle with him—a Winchester 30-30 lever action he had owned since he was a young boy. This gun was his pride and joy, and he never went on a hunt without it. Sometimes it would just stay in its case, but he knew it was there if he needed it. In this particular instance he had no intention of shooting at anything. The hunting and shooting would start when the rest of the guys showed up. It would be unfair to the others to get a head start, and this bunch of lunatics had more unwritten rules than a Las Vegas card dealer.

He was just going to look around for a while and make mental notes for future reference. A 10mm automatic pistol was with him—his own small cannon. Bush pilots in Alaska liked to carry this particular type of weapon in the event they should have an encounter with a large unfriendly animal when they are making deliveries in the wild. A person should always think twice before going into the deep woods—especially alone—without some sort of protective weapon. You never know what you may encounter.

* * *

The late afternoon sun was getting lower in the sky, a cool breeze was picking up. You could hear the rustling of dry leaves that still clung to the nearly barren trees. Jesse turned up the collar on his Carhartt jacket, leaving it just below his ears so he could hear, and shivered a little. He looked around, found a large tree stump with a clump of small evergreens nestled behind it, and sat down. *Perfect* he thought—*a good place to sit and listen for a while.* The best way to find out what's going on in the woods is to pick a good spot, sit down, and let the woods talk to you. There's a lot to be learned. The breeze had picked up making the trees sway and twist, occasionally rubbing together to make an eerie squeaking and groaning sound. A noisy red squirrel bounced back and forth in the trees above him warning the other animals of his presence. *Squealer* he said to himself with a smile. High above his head he could see hawks relentlessly circling, searching for food. Then all at once there was absolute silence—no birds singing, no squirrel chatter—something was about to happen. Suddenly a gun shot rang out and the bark on one of the evergreens behind him splintered.

In less than a heartbeat, Jesse's Army Ranger training kicked in. He hit the ground rolling, and was behind the stump in seconds, with his pistol in his hand. *What the hell is going on*, he thought. After a few long minutes, he managed to get his body high enough behind the stump to safely scan the area around him in search of whoever fired the shot. Jesse waited a few more minutes then thought to himself, *it's just just a hunter a little off target*. It happens now and then with new hunters that get a little over-anxious or excited when they see their first deer.

Of course there's some people who shouldn't be allowed to carry guns for any reason. *You can't cure stupid* Jesse thought to himself. Although feeling relatively confident there was no threat, Jesse kept a watchful eye as he headed for home. The sun was disappearing behind the treeline, and the beautiful fall moon appeared as Jesse entered his front yard. It would be dark soon, so it seemed like a good time to sit on the front porch and enjoy a tall strong drink. He figured while he was watching the fall moon flood the landscape, he would make mental notes about today's events and sightings.

Jesse sat in his favorite porch chair enjoying his drink, looking out over the fields into the treeline, trying to concentrate on the day's happenings. Although he tried hard, lately his thoughts kept wandering back to the wedding. The idea of hunting camp without Doc plagued him. He couldn't get what had happened to Doc out of his mind.

The whole scenario regarding the aftermath of the shooting

incident was a little hinkey as far as he was concerned. On several occasions, Jesse had made several attempts to contact agent Smith at the FBI. This was the agent Doc had told Jesse could be trusted, but he hasn't responded at all to Jesse's inquiry. All Jesse was trying to do was piece together the final outcome of the incident. He also wanted to find out what happened to Doc's remains. Had there been a service or a funeral? After many long weeks, Jesse finally received a formal letter from Agent Smith.

Agent Smith's apparent lack of concern toward the whole situation bothered him. He told Jesse that Doc had signed a waiver with the bureau, stating that in the event he was killed his body should be cremated and his ashes spread at sea, and that's what happened. Agent Smith wrote that there was little more to tell—Doc's wishes were fulfilled, the entire incident was a thing of the past and it was time for everyone to move on. This didn't sit well with Jesse, but what else could he do? *This isn't over yet*, he thought as he finished his drink. This is a good time to call Peppermint Patty about helping Peachy.

* * *

Jesse dialed up Peppermint Patty and was pleasantly surprised to have her answer on the second ring. He briefly explained to her how he was hoping she would be able to come visit his camp, and spend some time talking with Peachy. Just as Jesse expected, Patty's response was on a positive note, as always. She would be more than happy to come to camp and when did he want her there.

"Well," Jesse replied, "camp starts in three days. With any luck everyone will be here including Peachy, I hope." He still hadn't gotten a definite answer from Peachy.

Patty suggested that she call Peachy, to see if she could convince her to come and to offer her a ride.

"That would be great," Jesse answered, smiling to himself.

"Listen Patty, while you're at it, stop by Gretel's Cookie Crumbs, and see if you can get Linda Merten to come along too. Gretel was a good cook and a pretty darn good hunter. I know you two are pretty tight and with the whole gang here we could use a little help cooking. I have enough food supplies to feed a small army."

"Okay, Jesse, will do. I'll see you later tomorrow, should I bring a gun?" Patty said.

"Absolutely not," Jesse responded with a smile. Then he said to himself—*there's enough loonies out there. I don't need her to have a gun too.*

Jesse ended the call with Peppermint Patty, pleased with the fact she was willing to come to camp and talk to Peachy. *She's definitely a little out there*, he said to himself, *but is a cracker jack of a shrink. I hope she can help.* He decided to have maybe one more drink before bed.

Just as he started mixing, his cell phone rang. He checked the caller ID, and saw it was MJ. "Hey, where are you? I'm already two in," Jesse laughed.

"On my way—about thirty minutes out. I hope you don't mind but I have Squeaky Green with me," MJ replied. "She has some time off and said she could watch Neiko while I went into the woods."

"No problem—the more the merrier. Maybe we can give her some shooting lessons while she's here," Jesse answered.

"That's a great idea, Jesse. By the way, some asshole tried to run us off the road back in the Notch, and it was not by mistake either, it was definitely on purpose. I'll explain when we get there," MJ said.

The Notch is Franconia Notch Parkway in Franconia, New Hampshire. It's narrow two-lane stretch of road, surrounded by mountains. The only turnoffs are rest areas. This stretch of road has a speed limit of 45 miles per hour and for good reason. It can be particularly treacherous this time of year. The weather changes dramatically in the Notch due to the mountains. You get sun, rain, fog and snow at any time, day or night, making driving conditions dangerous and unpredictable.

"Those idiots are everywhere, MJ. Take your time and be careful, and I'll have one waiting for each of you when you get here." Jesse answered.

A little after 8:30 that evening, MJ, Squeaky, and Neiko arrived at the camp. The air temperature outside had dropped about twenty degrees, prompting them to quickly move inside. Clouds had overtaken the moon, and the wind was picking up, bringing with it some early snow. The trio of friends greeted each other warmly and sat in front of a blazing fireplace to help shake off the cold.

Jesse's fireplace was a very large center-of-the-room style that could accommodate a three-foot log easily, generating some serious heat if necessary.

While they sat around the fire enjoying their drinks together, Jesse brought MJ and Squeaky up to date on how he had called Peppermint Patty and asked her to try and convince Peachy to come to camp, with the hope that Patty could help Peachy heal some of her emotional pain. MJ and Squeaky thought this was a great idea, adding they would do all they could to help matters.

"If all goes well," Jesse said, "Patty should be here tomorrow sometime. She's also hoping to bring Gretel from Gretel's Cookie Crumbs, to help cook. Gretel can also get a little hunting in if she wants, or just have some time to relax. She's always been very good to us and has had a very busy summer. Now all we have to do is wait for Rick. I haven't heard from him—he could be anywhere."

"Yeah, as long as there's sun and golf," MJ laughed.

MJ had no sooner made the comment when there was a sharp rapping on the door. Jesse jumped up and opened it to find a New Hampshire State Trooper standing there with Rick. Jesse recognized the trooper as Mike Connors, a twenty-year veteran of the department, and an old friend. He had known Mike personally for over thirty years. They met when Mike was just a rookie in a small town, and was considering joining the state police. They soon became close friends.

"Hi Mike, what the hell's going on?" Jesse asked.

"Looks like someone doesn't like the way Rick drives," Mike smiled. 'They put his ass in the ditch, just inside the Notch by Echo Lake, I picked him up walking."

"Holy shit are you okay, Rick?" Jesse asked.

"I'm fine—that asshole better not let me get my hands on him," Rick growled. "My new clubs were in the truck, so was all my hunting gear, including my rifle and handgun."

"Just so you're okay is all that matters. We have plenty of hunting gear here, Arnold Palmer. Sit down by the fire and have a drink." Jesse said as he jokingly slapped his large friend on the shoulder. "Can I fix you one for the road, Mike?" Jesse asked the trooper.

"No thanks, Jesse, it's getting slippery out there. I better get going. Good luck with the hunt this year. Oh and by the way, sorry to hear about Doc—that really sucks." Mike replied, as he opened the door to leave.

"Thanks, Mike," Jesse replied, shaking Mike's hand and seeing him out the door.

Jesse dimmed the lights and the four friends sat around the fireplace talking about Rick's accident and how strange it was that MJ and Squeaky had almost been run off the road earlier in the day in the same area.

"You know guys, if I were paranoid, I'd think someone was trying to scare us," Jesse said. "Think about this! While I was out scouting today a shot went over my head and splintered a small hemlock right behind where I was sitting. Later someone tries to run MJ off the road, and the next thing you know, Rick gets run off the road. All this in the same day. What are the odds of that happening?"

"Maybe it's the deer," Rick yawned. "They're trying to scare the three amigos away. I'm beat. I'm ready to turn in."

—17—

Morning arrived, bringing a beautiful blue, cloudless, sunny sky. The ground had a light dusting of snow on it that sparkled in the sunshine, making the entire scene look like a winter wonderland. This was a hunter's dream, just enough snow to see the tracks left by the deer, making it easier to follow them into the woods.

"Wow! This is perfect, look at the tracks. There must have been a deer convention in the front yard last night," MJ shouted, as he stepped out the front door. Within a few short minutes, the door opened and MJ quickly came back in with a strange look on his face.

"What's wrong?" Rick laughed, "forget to put your shoes on? That's snow out there you know."

"Yeah and that's not all, whoever was looking in our windows forgot about the snow and left their footprints," MJ replied.

Rick went into the kitchen, where Jesse was starting to prepare breakfast, to let him know about MJ's discovery of footprints outside the camp windows and get an idea of what his thoughts were.

"Well, I guess my paranoia wasn't so far off about someone trying to scare us, let's just keep a lid on it so we can think about it for a while. Tell Squeaky and MJ not a word to the others, when they arrive we don't need to make them nervous," Jesse replied.

Breakfast was over and the sun was beginning to melt the light snow, making a nice early winter morning even nicer. The three amigos and Squeaky were sitting on the porch enjoying the morning when the quiet was interrupted by a four-wheel-drive vehicle racing up Jesse's more than a mile-long unpaved driveway at breakneck speed. He liked the distance from the main road— it gave him complete privacy, and no one can come up to the camp without being seen.

"Here comes that crazy shrink friend of yours, Jesse. I hope she puts the flaps down before she runs out of driveway," Rick said laughingly. The vehicle finally came to a sliding stop about thirty feet from the porch and the occupants sat there for a minute before getting out. Peppermint Patty was the first one out, followed by Gretel, Peachy, and to everyone's surprise and delight, Katie Burns, owner of Happy Valley Campground.

"Holy cow, this is great, the gang's all here," Jesse said, as smiles and hugs were exchanged all around. "How was the trip?"

"Actually, we were beginning to wonder if we would make it in one piece," Katie said, shaking her head and looking back at the road. "That was the ride from hell." Katie explained how things were going fine when they entered the Notch, traffic was very light and moving right along. Then all at once an oversized pickup truck came barreling out of one of the rest areas by Echo Lake, and got right on their rear bumper. She said the truck was so big and close, all you could see was the grill, and that it kept lightly bumping the rear of Patty's vehicle, trying to make them move over. Of course in the Notch, there's nowhere to move over so they had to speed up, as did the pickup, bumping them as they went. She said this continued until they were leaving the Notch parkway. Just as they were approaching the first off ramp, all at once the pickup suddenly swerved and took the exit, almost rolling itself over, while doing so. That's when the craziest thing happened. Patty told us the truck driver must have seen that Maine deputy sheriff, standing on the side of the road the same time she did, and decided to take off. We all looked at Patty like she was imagining things.

"What sheriff??" We all seemed to say in unison. No one had

seen anything or anybody, nevermind a Maine deputy sheriff in the middle of Franconia Notch Parkway in New Hampshire.

"Oh boy," Jesse said, shaking his head, "Let's go inside, you all know your way around. Find yourselves a room and get settled. I'll start a fire in the fireplace so we can gather round and get comfortable. There's also a few things I'd like run by everybody so we're all on the same sheet of music.

* * *

The afternoon sun was beginning to edge its way down in the western sky giving way to some darker wintry clouds. The group was all gathered in front of the fire reminiscing about old times and trash talking about the upcoming hunt. Katie and Gretel had just come into the room from the kitchen where they had been preparing a large dinner of chicken, ribs, and lasagna for later.

Jesse thanked everyone for being there and told them how happy he was that they all were able to come, and promised this was going to be the best hunting camp ever.

"There's just a few things of concern that I think everyone should be made aware of. As you ladies know quite well, it appears someone tried to force you off the road on your way here. And it just so happens someone tried to force MJ and Squeaky off the road while they were on their way here yesterday, and someone not only tried, but succeeded in running Rick off the road last night, forcing his truck into the water at Echo Lake. All three incidents happened not only in the Notch but in the same area. And, while I was out in the woods scouting yesterday, someone fired a shot at me or at least in my direction, hitting a tree behind me. I could see possible road rage in the Notch, if that's what it was, to happen once, but not three times. Particularly in the same area to people that just happened to be on their way here. Then top that off with someone shooting at me. I believe someone is either trying to scare the hell out of us or send us a message that we're a target. But if someone is really after us, this is the last place they should try. The outside walls of the camp are made of solid twelve-inch-thick logs that are sprayed every six months with fire retardant. The windows are bullet-proof glass, the roof is steel, and we have our own power and water supply plus plenty of food. That being said, let's just all do what we came here for—eat, drink, be merry—and watch me get the first deer," Jesse laughed.

That final comment was met with a round of boo's and laughter. Without a doubt, things were shaping up to be all that you would have expected when this group got together. Everyone had a great time singing, dancing, playing cards, charades, and teasing Rick about his truck being in the lake. Just after midnight the festivities came to a close and everyone except Jesse and Rick headed for bed. They were going to do a last minute check of the area. MJ has always said, if you look up the definition of paranoid or over-cautious, you will find a picture of Jesse and/or Rick. This comment comes from the guy that just slipped out of his room to join the other two in the darkened living room.

"Let's give it about an hour. Everyone would normally be asleep by then. I wouldn't expect anything while we're awake. What do you think?" Jesse asked.

"Sounds good to us. Are we going out, or using the cameras first?" MJ asked.

"I think that would be the best idea—use the cameras first so there's no surprises—then we can slip out the hidden door if we need to." Rick said.

When the camp was built, there was a hidden door installed that allowed you to exit without being seen. No one knew about this door except Jesse, Rick, and MJ. The only other person that ever knew about it was the original builder, Jesse's friend Danny the Lion, who was killed in Vietnam. The door is an undetectable moveable panel, located in the wall that houses the large center fireplace. The wall is approximately three feet deep, and it accommodates the wood box, bookshelves, various pictures, awards, and trophies that Jesse has collected. When the panel is slid open, it reveals an elevator capable of holding two people, allowing them to travel up inside the hollow wall, through the ceiling and exit at the cupola on the roof. This particular cupola, boasts a traditional ornamental wind direction indicator, and is mounted on a eight-foot-square platform, with decorative rails all around, giving it the appearance of a widow's walk.

The existence of an exit door built into the back of the cupola is impossible to detect.

Jesse activated the exterior motion cameras and the trio stood and watched the monitors, looking for any movement outside the camp. After an hour or more, without any activity. Jesse made sure the cameras were recording, turned to Rick and MJ and suggested they get some sleep. He then poured himself a drink and settled into his favorite chair by the fire.

* * *

Morning came with all its splendor, bright sunshine and a new dusting of snow sparkling like diamonds against the dark green hemlocks across the field. There had been no incidents during the night and everything appeared fine. Everyone sat around enjoying a big breakfast and discussing plans for the day.

"One more day before I shoot the first deer, so I think I'll go out and scout a little," MJ said.

This statement was first met with a resounding round of laughter, only to be interrupted by Peachy shouting out, "How much money are we talking, dog man?"

"Oh boy here we go," Katie whispered to Jesse and Rick with a big smile.

"Make it easy on yourself, how about anyone interested puts $50 in the pool. The first deer gets half, the biggest gets the rest?" MJ replied.

"You're on, Woof. Anyone else feel lucky?" Peachy asked, as she looked around the room with a big grin.

"I'm in," Jesse shouted.

"Me too," Rick chimed in.

"What about me?" Katie sputtered. "I've hunted before."

"Hey, count me in. I'll bait them with donuts," Gretel shouted.

Perfect, Jesse thought, as he looked around, smiling at his room-full of friends.

"Don't you even ask," he said to Peppermint Patty with a big smirk. "Well, gang, let's get out there and take a look around. Remember to take your cell phones and put them on vibrate so we can communicate with each other. Above all everyone, please be on guard for anything."

They all gathered in front of the camp and shared which direction each was heading in, just for safety's sake. Jesse pulled MJ aside and told him to shadow Katie without her knowing it. He then told Rick that they would take turns keeping an eye on Peachy, even though he was sure she could handle herself, and would probably sense they were there—she was really sharp.

They set off separately into the woods. The sun was high in the sky as they slowly crisscrossed the lower mountainside, following trails and sign left by the deer.

Jesse had just stopped to check a rub when he caught the glimpse of something shiny off on the side of the mountain above him.

"Shit! A scope!" he said out loud, as a shot rang out and the ground next to his feet burst up like a balloon. He instinctively dove for the cover of a downed tree as another, followed by a third shot, rang out splattering bark from the log in front of him. Jesse snatched his cell phone from a small pack he was carrying and sent out a text to the others. *Someone's shooting at me. Get back to the camp ASAP—stay alert—I'll be fine.* Immediate acknowledgment came back from the hunting party, along with a question mark from both MJ and Rick. Jesse texted back *don't worry, I got this*, as he snuggled tighter into the fallen tree.

MJ, Rick, and the others all made it back to the camp without incident and proceeded to explain to Peppermint Patty and Squeaky what had happened, and assured them Jesse would be fine. MJ further advised everyone to stay inside the camp.

* * *

The bright day had given way to late afternoon clouds, the sun was slowly sinking out of sight and there was a chill in the air. Jesse was snuggled in behind the fallen tree for protection. He had spent most of the afternoon scooping the dead leaves, loose dirt, and twigs away from the tree with his hands and a small stick, creating a shallow shelter from the wind and cold. It was a slow and tedious task—any kind of movement was kept at the minimum so it couldn't be detected by the shooter or shooters. *Let them think I'm dead*, he thought. As night fell and darkness enveloped the area, Jesse managed to reposition himself so he had a full view of the mountainside. *Now all I need to do is wait and hope for a moon*, he thought.

* * *

Meanwhile back at the camp MJ checked the outside cameras, in anticipation of Jesse's return. They were all concerned about his safety but were also positive he would prevail.

"After all, this isn't Jesse's first rodeo," Rick said with a grin. The evening went slowly. The group sat around taking turns checking the camera monitors, playing cards, and trying to stay calm.

Finally MJ announced, "I need a good strong drink right now, anyone else?" His question was answered with a resounding yes from the entire group. Even Gretel, who didn't drink, said yes. As MJ headed to the liquor cabinet, there was a solid thud sound on the camp door. Everyone froze right where they were and looked at each other. Rick jumped up and checked the cameras.

"Nothing showing in any direction," he said, as he took his .40cal pistol off the shelf by the fireplace, and headed for the door. MJ had already positioned himself with his pistol at the ready, anticipating Rick's reactions. Rick nodded to MJ and with one quick motion, pulled the door open. Nothing. No one there.

As Rick started to close the door, MJ said, "Holy shit, Rick look up." Over Rick's head embedded in the door was an arrow with a ziplock bag attached to it. Rick pulled the arrow out, stepped back closed and locked the door. They all stood looking at each other as if they were in shock.

"What the hell is in the bag?" Katie asked.

"It's empty," MJ said. Then he exclaimed, "Oh no it's not! There's a gray goose feather in there!" For half a second you could have heard a pin drop. Then from the other side of the room, Peachy came running and clutched the baggie MJ was holding, tears streaming down her face, sobbing uncontrollably.

"I knew it, I knew it! He's alive, guys! Doc's alive!" she stammered.

MJ and Rick looked at Peppermint Patty and in unison said, "You're mixing, make ours a double!"

"Mine too," Katie chimed in with a huge smile.

* * *

Up on the mountain Jesse was getting a little chilly as he waited patiently for the shooter or shooters to come and be sure he was dead. *You got the wrong guy* he said to himself. *I've laid in rain, mud, and filth a lot longer than this, with much fiercer adversaries than you trying to kill me. So bring it on assholes, whoever you are, you're gonna lose.*

The moon wasn't quite as bright as Jesse had hoped for, so he knew he would have to rely mostly on his hearing, if they approached. Just then—bingo! He heard a twig crack, then a small rustle of dry leaves. Jesse scanned the area the noise came from, remembering not to focus on one thing too long. Always look away then back, is how he was taught in ranger school. Nothing, then another noise in the same area. *I hear you* he said to himself, *keep coming*. A good half-hour passed with no further sounds. The breeze had come up, blowing some of the clouds away, allowing a little more moonlight to illuminate a figure with a rifle, advancing in his direction ever so slowly. Jesse waited patiently to see what the shooter's next move would be. At approximately twenty feet away the shooter raised the rifle and fired a shot into the tree trunk where Jesse had originally been shot at. Jesse sprang to his feet and responded with two quick shots from his 10mm handgun, hitting the center of the shooter's chest, sending them toppling over. The 10mm round hits its target at approximately 650-foot-pounds, so being hit by two rounds almost simultaneously is equivalent to getting hit by a small car. Jesse, shook his head and said, "I warned you," then quickly moved to another position and took cover, just in case there was another shooter.

* * *

Back at the camp it was chaotic. Tears, cheers, beers, skepticism, and everything in between. Katie and Gretel were the only two people that were acting normal, and that was marginal. Squeaky was passed out on the sofa. MJ was trying to have a meaningful conversation with Peppermint Patty, while Rick and Peachy sat in front of the fire, tears running down their cheeks, shaking their heads.

What a crazy night this has been. Just after midnight Rick's phone lit up. It was a message from Jesse. *I got one, not sure if there are any more. Do not respond, all okay here, will be in touch.* Rick and

Jesse had been through many dangerous situations similar to this one, so it was pretty hard to rattle them. They would just assess what was going on, adapt to whatever was happening, and react as necessary.

* * *

Dawn was breaking, bringing with it gray skies and a little blowing snow. Jesse was still in the same spot he had moved to after the shooting. He was tucked into some thick, low-hanging hemlock branches, that dangled down to within inches of the ground. The hemlock just happened to be next to a large tree that had blown over. It was a perfect spot. He had a clear view in all directions and a small stump, next to the tree, made a good seat. The only way he would be seen is if someone were to pull the branches back. Jesse waited for a while, then decided it was time to make a move. He slipped out of his hideaway and slowly made his way to the sprawled body of the shooter he had eliminated the night before. Carefully, he rolled the body over and was surprised to be staring into the face of Rocky Campbell, the former campground worker and female trafficker, who had been sent to prison.

Jesse was shaking his head in amazement. "I thought you were in prison," he said as he straightened up and then froze.

"*Was* is the key word," an unfamiliar female voice behind him said. "Now lose the gun tough guy and put your hands on top of your head with your fingers interlocked, or you'll be lying next to him."

Jesse dropped his 10mm handgun to the ground and put his hands on his head as instructed.

"Okay, let's go. Start down the mountain to the camp. Any false moves or funny business and you're dead," the voice said.

Jesse had no intention of trying anything as they headed down. He knew Rick would have the cameras on and be ready for their guest. *At least I hope so,* Jesse thought. Jesse continually tried to strike up a conversation, as they approached the camp, but the voice refused to answer. All he got in response was a gruff shut up and keep walking. *Who the hell is this?* Jesse wondered.

* * *

Meanwhile, Rick, MJ, and Peachy were monitoring the outside cameras looking for any movement or sign of Jesse. The wind and blowing snow that had started around dawn, was intensifying, making it more difficult to focus.

"Just what we need—not bad enough having the wind shake the cameras, and now the damn snow keeps sticking to the lens," MJ snarled.

"Relax, Woof," Peachy said to MJ in a low soothing voice. "We can do this and you know it. Jesse's fine."

Ever since the baggie with the gray goose feather had been found in the door, Peachy has had a transformation back to her old self—calm and calculating—with a tinge of fearless aggressiveness showing.

"Hey guys, look to the left side of your number 4 camera, it looks like a couple of hunters coming up the driveway and going into the woods. They're in cammies, have facepaint on and are carrying rifles. You guys see them?" Rick asked.

"I see them, but have a feeling they're not just hunters," Peachy chimed in. "One of us better try to keep them in sight."

"I'm on them," MJ said. "Oh boy guys, stand by, looks like two or three more coming. Not quite sure, with the damn snow blowing around. If they come a little closer before they go into the woods, I might be able to zoom in and get a better look at them."

Meanwhile, Jesse's captor had also seen the hunters entering the woods. She quickly instructed him to move into a dense group of hemlocks, had him sit on the ground, and then blindfolded him. She then took up a position situating herself and Jesse, inside the treeline, approximately 200 yards from the camp. From this location she could guard Jesse and still see the hunters if they were to approach. The hunters, who had now started to spread out, varied from 100 to 150 yards away from their location. They were moving back and forth, ever so slowly, not looking in any particular direction. It appeared they may have seen something on the ridge of the mountain and were heading that way. *What the hell is going on* Jesse thought, *I wish I could see—hope the guys back at camp are watching.* Jesse began slowly edging his hand toward his cell phone, only to be quickly warned that if he moved again he would die.

MJ had been working the camp security cameras back and forth trying to get the focus just right, so he could zoom in on the hunters and try to identify them.

Finally he got a clear picture, zoomed in and shouted, "Holy shit guys, it's those crazy gangster friends of Jesse's. I see Hawkeye, Wookie, Diamond Dave, Homeless Joe, and that one they call Giggles. I can't quite make out the last one, but believe it or not, I think it's Choo-Choo Charlie, Doc's buddy. Holy shit it is! That's one bad bunch of people."

Rick and MJ both looked at each other then over at Peachy, who was standing in front of the monitor nodding her head. She had a big smile on her face with tears running down her cheeks.

The sun was just setting an the wind had increased, making the woods noisy. Most seasoned hunters would sit and wait under these conditions. Even though things were far from perfect, several shots rang out and could be heard echoing from the mountainside. *Must be the hunters* Jesse thought, just as another shot ripped through the trees above them.

"That was close," Jesse said to his captor.

"It was closer than you think my friend," a familiar voice said, as his blindfold was untied and his 10mm pistol was dropped in his lap. Jesse jumped to his feet with tears in his eyes, as he looked into the face of his friend Doc. As the two old friends embraced each other, Jesse could see a black chopper rise up from the mountain above them, make a small tip to one side then disappear into the darkening night clouds.

"What took you so long?" Jesse said to Doc, with a mile-wide grin on his face and tears in his eyes.

Doc put his arm on Jesse's shoulder and said, "It's a long story my friend. Let's go down to the camp and I'll explain."

As they approached the camp Jesse texted MJ, *We're all set, the threat has been eliminated. I'm coming in. Find a reason to turn the cameras off for a minute, you'll see why when I get there.* Just as Jesse and Doc approached the edge of the driveway, Billy Murphy's pickup truck was pulling in with Billy, his wife Chloe, Eddie Bell, and Billy's dog, a black lab named Monback.

"Boy this is turning out great! The whole gang's here," Jesse said. Billy, Chloe, and Eddie climbed out of the truck, opened the tailgate and began unpacking their gear. Just as they finished unloading, they noticed Jesse walking in their direction with someone. The trio stopped what they were doing and stared in astonishment.

"Doc, is that you? We thought you were dead!" Billy shouted.

"Hey guys it's me. When we go inside, I'll explain what happened," Doc replied with a big smile.

The excited friends hugged Doc, gathered their gear and headed for the camp door, laughing and chatting. When they got to the door, Jesse held up his hand and motioned them to stop.

"Listen guys, wait here for a minute. I better prepare everyone inside for the news about Doc being alive, especially Peachy."

Jesse opened the door, quickly stepping inside. He was immediately greeted and surrounded by his friends. The questions came fast and furious, asking what happened out there, was he alright, who was shot, who were the hunters they had seen and where did they go?

Before Jesse could even begin to explain anything, Peachy

had pushed her friends aside, and was standing, looking Jesse right in the face. Tears were streaming down her cheeks, as she stammered, "Jesse, Doc's alive isn't he? We know it! We all saw the feather from the gray goose."

Jesse was completely caught off guard. He instinctively reacted without hesitation and blurted out, "Yup he's not only alive, but he's right outside that door waiting for you."

Peachy ran to the door, pulled it open, and found Doc standing there with open arms and a huge smile on his face. To say the scene was chaotic would be an understatement. There were cheers, tears, hugs, and everything else you could imagine. This great bunch of inseparable people was finally reunited again.

It was getting late, so they decided to wait until morning to try and completely explain in detail what had transpired during the last few months. In the meantime, they opened the liquor cabinet, broke out the bottles and celebrated well into the night.

—18—

Morning arrived. The skies were gray and the air was cold. Inside it was warm and cheery, and still bubbling with excitement over Doc's arrival. Everyone gathered around the large table for the traditional opening day breakfast. Doc explained to everyone that on the day of the wedding, he was not aware the bureau (FBI) had received a tip, helping them uncover a plot to have him and Peachy eliminated. It was discovered that Rocky Campbell, former female trafficker, had been released in the custody of a female FBI agent, to be transported to a hearing. It turns out there never was a hearing, the corrupt agent—the same one that Agent Smith and Doc had warned them about—along with Campbell—had planned the shooting well in advance. Certain higher government officials feared Doc and Peachy knew too much, and had to be taken out, once and for all. Unfortunately, before the bureau could act on the tip they had been given, the shooting took place. This caused them to immediately put a new plan in place. They had Doc declared dead, then removed him from the hospital to a secret location that boasted a full top of the line medical center. This location had been in existence for a long time. It was originally set up in the event this type of situation were to take place.

After his recovery, Doc was shipped to a secret location where he was debriefed, purposely leading him to believe that Peachy had not survived. His only contact during this time period was with fellow agents. It was suspected the shooters knew he was still alive and although they didn't know where he might be, they also knew his love for deer camp could be his demise.

Doc described how he had planned on surprising everyone on opening day, and had been tenting up on the mountain for about a week. He further explained he had no idea the shooters assumed his love for hunting camp would draw him out of hiding, and they would be waiting. While he was out scouting one day, he thought he heard voices and smelled smoke. So he quietly crept up on a small encampment, and discovered the presence of Rocky and the female agent. He said he heard them discussing how they would try separating the people coming to camp by running them off the road and or scaring them enough, so they would leave. If the plan worked and everyone didn't arrive, they would only have Doc to deal with when and if he came.

Without hesitation, Doc sent a message to his friend Choo-Choo Charlie, a former Delta Force member, requesting help. Charlie, being familiar with Jesse's friends from the other side of the tracks, contacted them, and described the situation. Without hesitation they arranged to meet him at the entrance to Jesse's camp. Then they would quickly and quietly eliminate any threat to Doc or the rest of the hunting party. The only hitch in the plan was when they missed the turn to Jesse's driveway. Hawkeye later told Charlie that if it wasn't for that Maine deputy sheriff pointing to the road, he would still be lost. Hawkeye said he really didn't quite understand what a Maine deputy sheriff was doing in New Hampshire, but he didn't have time to worry about it or stop to ask.

He went on to describe how they finally entered Jesse's property and headed up the mountain, pretending to be hunters. They explained they had also seen the female agent who had taken Jesse hostage, but did not acknowledge her. Instead they pretended to be looking elsewhere, and walked on by. Much later in the day, as the sun was going down, they began firing some random shots for distraction purposes only. This was all according to plan, allowing Charlie time to do what he does best.

His Delta Force training makes him a very dangerous and formidable opponent, and not one to take lightly. His ability to creep up on the enemy and subdue them before they react is renowned through the agency. In this case he didn't fail. He quickly and quietly ended the female agent's life. Then along with help from the others, removed her body, along with Rocky's, to the waiting chopper. They quickly gathered their gear, climbed on board, and left for places unknown.

After he finished filling everyone in on what had happened, Doc reassured them there was nothing more to be concerned about. He told them that a special team of agents had been on board the aforementioned chopper, and made sure the entire area was clear before leaving.

Then, with a smile, he said, "As far as the powers that be are concerned, this whole incident never happened. There could be one little problem, he conceded. Heaven forbid that the nosey damn reporter, Windy Chase from WHEIDI, caught wind of it. It appears she was reporting on a pickup truck that was found in the lake off the Franconia Notch parkway, so be prepared." He reminded everyone how Windy had stuck her nose in where it didn't belong in a case they had been working on, involving the missing teen named Susan, creating some confusion for the investigators.

Doc turned to Jesse and proposed a toast to the anxious group of hunters. After the toast, Jesse, with a mile-wide smile, announced, "Hunting camp is officially open, gang! Let's hit the woods."

Katie and Gretel were the first ones out the door, and in less than ten minutes, two quick shots rang out. Jesse and the rest of the group rushed out on the porch to see what was going on. They saw Katie and Gretel standing at the edge of the field waving wildly, pointing to an eight-point buck and a very large doe, lying at their feet.

"Here we go, gang! Happy hunting!" Jesse shouted. *Perfect*, he said to himself with a smile, as he turned and went inside. "I guess I better get my gun. You ready for this, ghost?"

ODE TO THE GHOST

ALTHOUGH HIS TIME ON EARTH IS DONE
HE'S OFTEN SEEN IN UNIFORM
GUIDING THE PEOPLE HE HELD SO DEAR
THROUGHOUT THE SHORT TIME HE WAS HERE
SO HERE'S TO DAVE OUR GLASS WE RAISE
TO TELL HIS TALES AND SING HIS PRAISE
THE CAPTAIN OF THE CAMP PATROL
WHO'S TRULY MISSED
BY ONE AND ALL.

Made in United States
North Haven, CT
03 May 2024